S0-AHY-959

CK

THE WHITE RAVEN

SUE COLEMAN

Copyright © 2019 by Sue Coleman
First Edition - 2019

ISBN : 978-0-9948321-1-5

www.suecoleman.ca
email: Sue@suecolemabn.ca

All characters in this book are fictitious,
and any resemblance to actual persons, living
or dead, is purely coincidental.

All rights reserved
No part of this publication may be reproduced, stored in a
retrieval system, or transmitted in any form or by any means,
electronic, mechanical, photocopying, recording or otherwise,
without the prior permision of the author.

Printed and bound in Canada by Friesens

Thanks goes to my good friend and mentor Terry who pushed me into thinking outside the box, corrected my terrible run-on scentences and did his best to stamp out the cliches. Also my brother, Dave, for correcting the worst of my punctuation and his advice on fonts and layout.

For all my grand children
I hope you enjoy it.

1
The Spider and the Fly

Raven sat perched halfway up his favourite cedar tree, bored beyond reason.

Bzzzzzz. Bzzzzzz.

An angry buzz sounded above his head.

Why is it, when life is easy and you have no problems to solve, everything becomes dull and uninteresting?

BzzzzTzzzz. Bzzztzzz.

Fidgeting on his perch, he twisted his head sideways, the light bouncing off his black feathers in rays of green and purple. He squinted, making the scenery a fuzzy blurr.

Bzzzzz. Bzzzzzz.

He relaxed his eye muscles, refocused, and reality flooded back into his brain. From this angle he could see a spider's web strung across the branch just above his head.

Bzzzzzz

Struggling in the middle of the strands was a large black fly. Raven's boredom made him irritable and the frantic buzzing of the fly drilled into his senses until he thought his skull would explode. He snapped the bug in his strong beak, crushing it into silence. Then, with a flick of his head, he tore the remains of the web to shreds.

"Now, was that totally necessary?" A sharp voice rang down.

"I spent a good part of the night building that one." Peering into the tangled branches, Raven spotted a tree spider clinging to a broken thread that swung back and forth above his head.

"Bad enough you eat my breakfast. No respect these days. Willful destruction of other people's property, I just can't believe it. Didn't your parents teach you anything?"

Frustrated at losing such a juicy snack, the spider threw caution to the wind, or in this case the breeze. His natural, inborn fear of large birds with healthy appetites had vanished when the fly disappeared into the raven's beak.

"Hours of work, not counting the planning and careful placement of the foundation strands. Then there was the traffic analysis, wind funnel assessment, and the elemental protection survey, all destroyed with a snap of a beak. YOUR beak."

It would take the spider another full day to clean up the mess and reconstruct the web. The chances of catching another bug as big as that bluebottle was slim. It had created such a racket, sending out enough danger signals to warn traffic away from this branch for days. No, he'd have to move on, and that made for a very angry spider.

"Well, where for spirits sake were you?" Snapped Raven. "The damn thing was annoying. It's been buzzing for ages."

"I was busy," snapped back the spider. "There was no rush, that web was one of my best, built strong enough to last for days. That fly wasn't going anywhere. It had no chance of escape 'till you came along and stole it. I bet you weren't even hungry."

Truth be known, the spider had been sleeping. After a long night he was overtired. Which, in case you hadn't noticed, is when you get your worst nightmares. Even a minute brain is capable of an imagination, albeit rather limited. A spider's brain focuses on flies, but one big enough carry you off and inject eggs into your carapace, that will hatch into maggots, is a spider's worst nightmare. With his mind caught up in fighting with his own imagination, it had taken a while before his senses had separated the buzzing fly in the web from the horrible drone of the monster's wings in his dream. That snooze had cost him a night's work, his breakfast, all that planning, and . . . and . . .

The spider's mandibles twisted in frustration and a thousand complex eyes scowled at the raven, who was beginning to feel rather uncomfortable. Raven felt the mass of pinpricks as the hate built up in each pupil. Next it would be lighting bolts.

"I didn't eat it."

"What do you mean 'you didn't eat it?' I saw you."

Raven sighed. "You saw me kill it. I didn't eat it. I dropped it. It's probably stuck on one of the branches down there somewhere."

The spider was so shocked he garbled his words.

"You mean to say you threw it away? Wanton destruction of property, stealing the very food that another creature depends upon for survival, and then just tossing it aside with complete disregard . . ."

He dropped a few inches on his thread.

"I don't believe it . . ."

He dropped again.

"The waste . . ."

He dropped.

"Some creatures . . ."

He was now several feet below the raven, still he dropped, and still he ranted.

"No consideration . . ."

"None at all . . ."

Raven shook his head and sighed. What was his world coming to? Here he was, arguing with a spider. There was a rustle and a small twig snapped on the branch behind him.

"Tell me I didn't hear what I just heard."

Raven peered around the trunk of the cedar.

"Not you too."

Sure enough, Bilgat, a small eagle with bright penetrating eyes, was cleaning his talons.

I know, you're going to tell me that eagles and ravens don't mix. Well, to human ears, spiders don't talk either. So, what's your point?

Muscles don't count for much in today's modern world. It's what's up top, under that cranial dome that matters. A very modern eagle was Bilgat, the great, great, grandson of Great Eagle. The same Great Eagle who had flown the skies with Raven's long departed ancestor.

Circumstances, and Raven's quest to understand the spirits, had thrown the two birds together. Now they were a team. Well, almost. They were definitely becoming close associates, an item, at least in the eyes of the inhabitants of the bay.

Situated on the protected, inside shore of Vancouver Island, off the west coast of Canada, a narrow sheltered bay takes a bite out of the shoreline. Behind it, a warm valley cuts deep into the backbone of the island and ends at a very large lake. A river winds like a snake from the lake, through the valley, and ends up emptying itself onto the tidal flats of the bay, then into the sea.

A small village and marina nestle on the southern shore of the bay, whilst on the north side is a steep mountain. At the foot of the cliffs a few houses are scattered on land that had once been the site of a thriving native village.

The long houses have gone, their totem poles carried off to some museum, and only a few families remain. Still, Raven thought of them as 'his people'. Although

---

over the past few years his thoughts hadn't been too fond.

Time and modern science have changed the people. They no longer believe their own legends and they have turned their backs on his ancestor. The old stories are forgotten. The young people no longer look up to Raven, the creator, the transformer, the trickster, the bringer of the light. Those days are gone. In today's world, creation is in the hands of machines. Computers are the transformers, the government is now the trickster and a man called Thomas Edison brought the light.

So where does a bird fit in?

If you've already read my last book, "Return of the Raven" you're probably getting impatient about now and want to get on with the story, but be patient, there may be a few who haven't, and for those of you who haven't, now would be a good time to slip out and beg, borrow or, heaven forbid, buy it, because the answer is too big to fit into one chapter let alone a paragraph.

I'll make it short, but you'll have to read my last book to fill in the details.

The spirits returned.

Huh, what do you mean 'is that it?'
I told you, go read the book.
Now where was I?

Bilgat squinted at Raven.

"You've been sitting here huddled in this tree all morning. You need to get out and catch some fresh breezes or you'll end up with tree fever."

Raven scowled. "S'all right for you to talk, you don't get gulls following you all over the place. I can't get a moments peace. It's enough to make me go crazy. Look at them out there, just waiting for me."

He flicked his head toward a flock of gulls gathered at the water's edge. The eagle's sharp eyes studied them. To him they didn't look any different from any other group of gulls. Some were staring off at the horizon, the rest pecked at odd bits of weed and shell in a halfhearted hope of finding a juicy tidbit.

Bilgat shook his head, "I think you're letting the dark winter skies get to you. You need to lighten up a bit."

"That's a rather odd choice of words considering." Suspicion crept into Raven's eyes as he scowled at the eagle knowing that, like most eagles, he was clairvoyant. "You bin mind reading again?"

"No I haven't. Why?"

"Because I feel like there is a big black cloud slowly creeping up from somewhere. I know the sky is clear at the moment, but it's as if there is a big storm coming. I started to feel it weeks ago. Now it's getting worse. It's as if a mouse is trying to build a nest in my head."

Bilgat studied the raven, taking great care in choosing his next words.

"Maybe you need to get away for a bit. Things are running pretty smooth around here. A trip might do you good. Put things in perspective."

"You think I need a holiday?"

"Well, you said it not me. Actually, I think you need to do something to take your mind off all this spirit stuff. It's getting you depressed. Look, I'm going up to the lake to see if I can spot a nice trout. When you've finished dealing with whatever it is you're doing, why don't you join me for an early supper. Things always look brighter after a good meal."

With that Bilgat took to the sky, swooping down to the water's edge, scattering the line of gulls.

For the first time that day, a twinkle crept into the raven's eyes as he watched the gulls flee in panic.

Bilgat turned inland, vanishing over the tree tops. Meanwhile Raven settled back on his branch and let out a long sigh, the type of sigh that carries the weight of the world on its wings. Things were changing, he knew it, could feel it, and it wasn't just the ominous feelings. There was something else. The spirits had returned, he knew that, but somehow he felt that things were . . .

Odd?

No.

Out of place?

No.

Off the flight path?

No.

Well what then?

He didn't know.

Voices that weren't there.

Invisible voices that seemed to know his thoughts.

Sure that makes a lot of sense, no wonder he felt irritable. No wonder he was sitting talking to himself.

Why me? He never asked the spirits to work through him.

Didn't you?

The thought seemed to come from deep within the very heart of the tree itself.

"Well I didn't expect it to be like this."

The branch he was perched on quivered.

What did you expect?

"Honour, respect . . ."

You have to earn that.

"I suppose fixing the bay and saving the salmon doesn't count for anything?"

One good chapter in a book doesn't make a best seller.

"Pardon?"

Sorry . . . a bird can't fly with only one feather in it's wing.

"Huh? And the seagull and goose? Oh and don't forget mister high and mighty eagle."

You need a lot of feathers to fly.

"So what am I supposed to do? Go out and fix the whole world?"

Oh for beaks' sake, he thought, now here I am talking to a blasted tree. His claws gripped the branch so tight they penetrated the bark.

A tremor ran down the tree to it's deepest roots, then spread out through the soil, clay and bedrock to the very shell of the turtle's back.

The turtle moved his feet.

* * *

Legends tell that mud was spread on the back of the great sea turtle. It became the first land and seeds, brought up from the bottom of the ocean, were planted. When we have an earthquake it is because the turtle gets tired and has to move its feet.

* * *

Above, in the ozone layer two spirits watched.

Did we make a mistake?
We do not make mistakes
Then have we returned too soon?
Maybe too late.
Give him time. It was the most balanced division of the life
force we have ever achieved in an egg.
Dividing an egg? Are you saying he had a twin?
Yes. He had a brother.
Where is he?
Banished. It was before your time.
What happened?
It is a long story
We are not going anywhere.

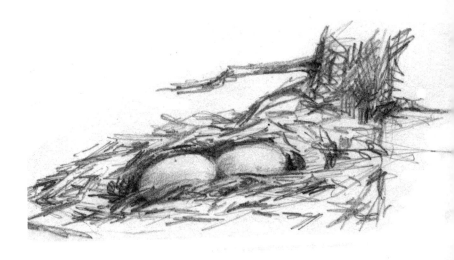

2
Banished

Far to the north, and
several hours flight west
from the main coast, is a small island.
It is surrounded by a group of ugly, jagged rocks that
rise like a wall out of the sea.

Years and years of the sea breaking over them, with
all the fury that the west coast weather can create, had
only served to sharpen them, turning them black with
algae. Boats stayed clear of the area and even the sea-
life made a wide circuit.

Within the craggy barrier, mist shrouded the land.
The clouds hung, like a heavy blanket, trapped just

---

above the scrubby bushes and straggly, windswept trees. Eerie tendrils of damp, cold fog drifted down through the branches, making everything wet.

At the northern tip of the island, the land rose, ending in a precipice. Winter gales had shaped and carved the black sandstone bluffs into elaborate rock sculptures, that, with a little imagination, formed strange, ghostly, twisted bodies.

The water below the cliff was smooth, with barely a ripple breaking the surface. Even during the worst storm, the outer reef protected these waters. They were deep and black, mirroring the rock face and, as the tide rose, the strange shapes joined with their reflections all along the base of the cliff. The result resembled totem poles, a bilateral symmetry of eyes, beaks and wings. The eyes watched.

At the top of the cliff is an ancient, weather beaten snag. So old and twisted by the north wind, it is hard to identify what type of tree it had once been. There is no colour left in the limbs as the bark was stripped off long ago. It is as white as the mist that wraps around it so that the bird that sits hunched in its branches seems to be floating in mid air.

The bird is a raven.

At first glance you might not see him. Just like the branches, he blends well with the mist.

A white raven.

One with an extremely bad attitude.

Not that you could really blame him, stuck as he is on this godforsaken island out in the middle of nowhere. Trapped and with no hope of escape.

How and why? You may well ask.

Since the beginning of time there have been ravens, very smart birds, the bird chosen by the spirits. As the years passed and the mortal body of the chosen aged, the need arose for a replacement. One very special egg was laid, from which hatched twin chicks. From birth it was obvious one was much stronger; although he was also clumsier and prone to doing rash things that seemed quite foolish. As the two grew and the pinfeathers started appearing, the distinction between the two became obvious. One had beautiful rich dark black feathers, the other was white.

Over the years, in an effort to find a perfect disciple, the spirits had divided yolks at conception. Doing their best to create a bird that was pure in thought, one that would allow them to return to the world. With ravens, that can be a difficult task and, over time, the spirits discovered it was almost impossible. Subject to temptation and greed, raven after raven failed in expectations. Pure doesn't come into a raven's vocabulary, however, the spirits' efforts were not without some successes.

As usual they got their colours backwards. Spirits have no concept of colour. The white raven absorbed the meanness of the two. Although it's hard to perceive one raven being any greedier than another, the white raven was. He was also bigger, faster and stronger. That's the problem with trying to create pure, it's nearly always weaker. You need some wicked in the mix for strength and perseverance. Call it character if you want, but you still need it. Getting the right mix into the black raven was a challenge but, over the years, the spirits had narrowed it down. This last hatching showed the most promise yet.

They waited and watched.

Things often happen fast. Once a dam is broken it's hard to hold back the flood. The spirits had finally found a black raven that listened and they were excited.

When times are good it is easy to forget the bad. It was necessary to banish the white raven to be sure he didn't corrupt his brother.

The trap was always the same.

Such an easy task.

Greed was his downfall, a small hint of unlimited food, and wealth beyond his wildest dreams, sent on the wind was all that was needed to entice the white raven north and across the ocean to this deserted pinnacle of rock.

Once across the surrounding reef, the guarding spirits rose and trapped him. Every attempt at crossing back failed, his wings were drained of strength and barely kept him aloft long enough to return to the safety of the beach. White Raven was strong but the spirits were stronger. Eventually he stopped trying.

With the evil brother safely out of the picture, the spirits relaxed, and, as our hero, the black raven, grew to a mature bird, they watched and waited.

Then came the day when Raven tried his best to help a dying frog, tentatively the spirits had reached out.

White Raven was forgotten.

The problem is, the bad very rarely forgets. Quite the opposite in fact, it not only remembers, it builds resentment. The white raven hated the island. He hated the mist. He hated the meager scraps of food that washed up on the shore but most of all; he hated the spirits that had trapped him here. He breathed hate until it became bitterness, resentment, and finally blinding white rage. He rotated the different moods through the different days of the moon. It broke up the monotony.

Today White Raven sat huddled on his branch his wings forward, his shoulders hunched, in an attempt to keep his chest warm. Over the last few months he had a feeling things were changing, something was different. Oh, the mist still hung in the trees, the waves still burst against the rocks, breakfast was the same old mouldy, soggy bread crust that the gulls had ignored, and lunch, a fish carcass so bloated it was hard to recognize the species. As usual the eyes were gone. He had forgotten what eyes tasted like, but he knew they were the best part.

Eyes. Something clicked in his memory.

Eyes?

That was it.

His head swiveled and his dark pupils fixed on the reflections at the base of the cliff. That's what was missing, the eyes.

He stretched his neck and peered further over the rim of rock. The shapes were still there, wings, beaks, legs, but no eyes. No eyes staring up from the depths of the inky black water. No eyes watching.

White Raven slowly lifted one claw then the other and worked his way along the branch until he reached the splintered end. From here he could see further around the twisted columns of sandstone, but still no sign of the eyes.

With effort, he stretched his wings. The damp air caused his joints to ache and lack of use had weakened his muscles. All the years of hopping and flapping his way around this miserable rock left him badly out of shape.

Putting some effort into a halfhearted flap he plunged into the mist. His soggy feathers dragged him down as he twisted his tail just enough to force his body into a glide along the face of the cliff. He flapped and floundered around the islet once, then twice. He would have done a third circuit if his wing tips hadn't been throbbing so badly that, with each down beat, it felt as if he was being pounded with hail stones. Stones so icy cold they burned. Finally he landed on a slimy, wet, weed covered clump of rocks by the beach. His whole body shook from the exertion and he wheezed and panted for ages. All the while his mind was in turmoil.

The eyes were not there. For every waking moment since his entrapment all those years ago, the eyes had watched. At first he had screamed at them and plunged his beak into the icy waters in an attempt to pluck them out. As quickly as his beak had broken the surface, the eyes had closed and vanished, only to appear again as soon as the ripples smoothed and the water calmed.

In a rage he had spent days throwing stones into the water, but after he was exhausted, the eyes returned. He had eventually managed to live with them by turning his back to the ocean and not looking into its depths. The only trouble with that solution was that the rest of the island became a cruel reflection of how he felt; miserable, miserable scraggy trees and even more miserable rocks. Most of the time he just shut his eyes, hunched down on the only limb that was strong enough to hold his weight, on the only dead snag on the whole rocky, forsaken island.

Where had the eyes gone? More important, when had they gone? He couldn't remember when he had last looked.

Well they're gone now.

Yes, but for how long? His mind raced.

Was there a chance that he could actually get off this blasted rock?

His eyes looked out, across the waters toward the mainland; the coastline that taunted him, calling to him in his exile. Even through the mist he knew which direction it was, and it was a good day's flight at the very least.

He vaguely remembered the trip that brought him here so long ago when he had been younger and a lot stronger. It was a long flight then, it certainly wouldn't be any easier now.

Well, if there was even the slightest chance, he would take it, or die in the attempt. He was sick of this life. He flapped his wings again, a thread of hope giving them renewed strength. He glanced in the direction of the sun. It was a misty, sickly green-yellow patch that didn't even attempt to penetrate the fog. Where had the day gone? Even though winter was finally past, the days were still short this far north, and soon the dark of the night would start creeping out from the hidden crevasses in the cliff.

One part of White Raven's brain wanted to fly now, this very minute, immediately even; whilst he still had the chance. The other half, the scheming and conniving half, looked back at the water-with-no-eyes and told him he needed to rest. He needed to gather his strength if he was to make it back. If two trips around the island had him this tired, he had little hope of making it to the coast. He needed to think. He needed to plan.

Over the years he had managed to hoard quite a few bits and pieces, treasures that had drifted in with the tides. Maybe amongst them he had something that would help him get off this rock.

He flapped his way to a deep, half hidden crevice that he had discovered long ago during a particularly wet and miserable night, and squeezed in through the narrow crack in the cliff face. Inside, it was reasonably dry. It was the one and only place on the whole island where the mist failed to penetrate. Scattered around the small cave was his hoard. A vision had brought him to this forsaken place promising riches. Instead all he had were a few bottles with soggy scraps of paper in them and a scattered selection of bits from old shipwrecks. Even so he studied them all carefully, his creative mind weighing up their value.

An old paddle, hmmm . . . no good without a boat.

Bits of broken glass, mostly blue, his favourite . . . no help there.

An old canvas sheet, probably from the sails of a sunken galleon, hmmm, maybe . . .

Then there were the piles of coloured nylon rope, the type that floats, that were carefully colour coordinated and placed around the walls to try and give the cave a cheerful homey atmosphere. The bits of seaweed and barnacles that were attached to most of the strands spoiled the effect, but they did provide a convenient snack on those days, when he didn't want to step outside, which was most.

White Raven had spent many winter evenings untangling the ends of the ropes, and then re-tangling them so they stayed together. Lots of little pieces of rope, joined together, made longer pieces of rope. He had gotten quite good at it, and was proud of his collection.

His eyes continued around the cave to the very far corner. There, carefully piled were his favourite treasures. His glass ball collection. Everything here had floated in with the tides.

Everything around him floated.

Pity Ravens didn't.

But what if . . . he looked again his eyes searching

his collection. Hope set his pulse racing. Yes, he could
see it, all he needed was . . .

He started scratching furiously in the sand, creating,
designing.

As night fell across the
island and the
mist dissolved
into the inky
blackness,
White Raven
planned
his escape.

3
Escape

Back in the valley, grey morning clouds were collecting along the top of the mountain ridge. They now decided to move in on the bay. It was a joint effort, and Raven's self pitying mood was broken with the first drops of rain hitting his beak. The wind, always quick to rise to the occasion, was steadily building strength and, as usual, was full of enthusiasm. As the last few remains of the spider's web were torn from the branches, Raven decided a trip inland was not such a bad idea. Maybe Bilgat had caught his fish by now. A nice juicy fish head might help lift his spirits, but he had his doubts. The look of the clouds as they loomed ominous overhead told him that, before too long, things were going to get quite uncomfortable around here.

Raven spread his wings and allowed the gusts to carry him across the water before he turned inland. A glance back and he saw the rain coming down the mountainside. Already the tops of the surrounding hills were hidden in the downpour.

Not a moment too soon, he thought.

He flew up river, over the roof of the old mill, and headed toward the lake. The trees had not yet completely filled out with new leaves but the maples were covered with hanging bunches of golden flowers. The air, filled with yellow clouds of pollen, smelled sickly sweet from the new growth on the cottonwoods. The warm sunny days of summer were a long time coming this year and today it still felt like winter. The mood of the weather certainly matched the mood of the raven; in fact it was so well matched that it might make you pause to wonder about the laws of cause and effect.

The closer Raven flew toward the lake, the weaker the winds became. Just as he thought, a sea squall, born where the sky meets the sea. Bad tempered and totally unpredictable except in one thing, a fear of traveling too far from their birthing grounds. Their obvious pleasure at striking fear into anything on or near the water was legendary as they raged across the water sucking up the waves and ripping their tops to shreds, leaving behind trails of foam. In the summer months they lurked behind islands or hung out in the mouth of inlets, but in the spring and fall they gathered above the hills and forests that surrounded the bays challenging each other to shows of strength. The resulting storms would be fast and furious, tearing through the trees, flying out over the water, raging at each other till one or the other finally weakened and died. The victor would swirl around in a triumphant circle before returning to the top of the cliffs to wait for the next challenger. When the clouds gathered, even the gulls flew inland.

As he flew up the valley, Raven searched the landscape, but apart from a small group of gulls huddled together on the sheltered side of one of the farmer's fields, nothing seemed out of place, yet the ominous feelings didn't stop. Somewhere, something was not right, he could feel it. There was an irritating little niggle in the back of his brain telling him that before too long his life was going to be extremely uncomfortable, and it had nothing to do with the state of the weather.

The image of a nest and broken eggshells flashed through his head. As fast as it came it was gone. In mid flight Raven shuddered. He could still feel the pain of those spiteful pecks from his brother to the top of his head.

What on earth had brought that on?

The White Raven

Far to the north we find White Raven on a pitiful little beach; barely a crack in the rock face. Fine white sand, the product of years of eroding barnacles, line the narrow inlet. There is just enough room for a bird to spread his wings, but the one good thing about the beach is that it is far enough back into the rocks to be out from the sight of the eyes, should they return.

White Raven laid out the ropes, placing them with care, overlapping each and fanning them out like a web. On top of these he dragged the canvas sheet, going around afterwards correcting all the ropes where the canvas had dislodged them. Then he rolled down his glass balls, one at a time, placing them in the centre of the canvas, the largest to the outside, the smallest to the middle, like eggs in a nest.

It was a struggle to lift the sheet corners over the balls, first one corner . . . rest . . . then the next . . . rest, until they were all wrapped up in an envelope of canvas. There were rivet holes along the canvas edge and White Raven wove a thin piece of line through them, poking it in one hole then pulling it through to the next, moving around the canvas from corner to corner. It took a long time and used up nearly all his lengths of rope but finally he was finished. Then he took all the ends and pulled them to the top of the bundle. Each one he entwined and twisted together; all those long evenings, weaving and braiding rope had made him an expert. At last they were all tangled into one great big colourful, and somewhat artistic, knot on top of the wrappings. His last trip back to the crevice was not to say goodbye but to grab the paddle in his beak.

He placed the paddle on top of the wrappings hooking it into the ropes. Finally he hopped back and studied at his creation. It looked odd, not quite what he had envisioned. He flapped his way around checking

---

each fold of the canvas and twist of the ropes, tightening and tucking till eventually he realized there was nothing more he could do except wait for the tide.

The ink black water was creeping up the beach. It wouldn't be long. White Raven paced; patience was not something he was good at. Every so often he hopped to the entrance of the cut and checked the water at the base of the cliff, afraid that the eyes might, even now, have returned to prevent his escape.

As the waters rose, he became more and more agitated and, when it started to lap around the base of the first canvas wrapped ball, he put his head down and using all his remaining strength, gave the raft a mighty shove.

The forces of nature will not be hurried and White Raven sat back nursing his beak, sullen, watching as the water continued to sneak up and around his makeshift raft. It gurgled in glee as it lapped at White Raven's feet, seeming to sense his frustration. Time slowed whilst the ink black waters crept. At last the cloth started to move, the glass balls inside began to float. The fabric undulated with each ripple as though taking in long, great breaths of air. The raft came to life.

White Raven hopped on top of the bundle. It held. He waited until, finally, the water completely covered the small beach. Taking the paddle in his beak he probed the water behind the raft, it was getting deeper and deeper. Suddenly the raft moved and the white raven was adrift. He flapped his wings and the bundle moved out of the shelter of the cliff. Using the oar as a rudder, he steered the craft across the ominous black expanse toward the gap in the rocky reef.

It was early evening; working all day, White Raven was obsessed with just one thought, escape. The wind dropped and the waves calmed for the night. It was stealthy quiet and silence hung heavy. The only sound was the whoosh of air created by each down beat of White Raven's wings. Although tired, the excitement gave him strength. Pent up anger and frustration gave him the determination to succeed, and the raft slid through the gap.

Outside the reef, the current was strong. For many years the raven had watched driftwood rush past, caught in the grip of the tidal flow. He knew it flooded south, and south was where he wanted to go, but he needed to get out as far as possible, away from the reef or he would end up smashed to pieces on the rocks at the south end of the island. He also needed to get far enough out so there was no chance of a back eddy pulling him out of the flow, sending him back to the shore, or at least, not this shore. So he continued to flap, and flap, and flap till he was exhausted. Taking a short break he looked back. The island was still too close. Years of hate fuelled his wings. Adrenaline forced them to flap mechanically. Pain from his screaming muscles fired him on, and finally, as the island slowly blended with the horizon, he collapsed into a fitful stupor. He was free.

4
The Owl

Raven circled the southern shore of the lake several times, his sharp eyes searching for Bilgat. Quite a few other birds had also traveled inland, looking for protection from the storm so the shoreline was unusually crowded. There was no sign of the small eagle. It was getting late in the day, Raven had had no lunch and the light was starting to fade along with the hope of a fresh evening meal.

So much for the spirits, he thought, they obviously didn't concern themselves with feeding the flesh. He flew down to the waters edge and took a long drink. From the corner of his eye, he spotted a small movement in the sand and, with a quick snap of his beak, he crushed a small crayfish. The sparkle returned to his eye as he swallowed, all the while searching the base of the reeds for more. Within seconds he spotted another, then another. Maybe the spirits had heard his need after all. Never before had he managed to find and catch a meal with such ease. He worked his way along the bank, eating his fill, until he came to the foot of a giant cedar, a mighty redwood.

There were none of these trees left back in the bay, but here in the valley a few stood, as a reminder of how things had once been during his great grandfathers time, before the pale skinned people cut them down for their mills.

The mighty cedar, the tree of life, was a very suitable place to spend the night. The great branches dipped in curving arcs as the weighty limbs were pulled down by the force of mother earth. At the same time, a life force flowed through them to their young green growth that struggled, reaching up towards the life-giving sunlight. Curtains of moss hung throughout the tree. Yes, it would be a very comfortable night.

Raven flapped his way through the branches that were so widely spaced he hardly brushed them with his wing tips, and finally settled on a comfortable moss covered branch. As he peered into the gathering gloom, he saw he was level with the tops of the surrounding cottonwood trees, even though he was still far from the top of the cedar.

For the first time that day, he felt comfortable. The annoying niggles in his gut had receded. Maybe it had just been hunger after all. He pushed the small nagging doubt to the back of his mind, determined to have a good night's sleep.

"Welcome." A soft, deep female voice startled Raven and pulled him back from the dark edges of oblivion. "Raven, Son of Raven, sleeping in my tree. Who, hoo would have believed it? I'll be the talk of the family nest."

Raven forced his eyelids open. There, sitting directly across from him was a fairly young, but very beautiful bird. Her soft, sad brown eyes were focused on her visitor, studying him carefully.

"I'm sorry, Miss, you have the advantage. I don't believe we've met," he tried hard not to yawn, "Yet you know my name." Raven shook off the grasping wisps of the night and sighed. Sleep would have to wait. Just his luck to choose a tree that was home to an owl, the harbinger of death. For those that believe in the stories; when an owl flies overhead, someone is soon to die.

A soft gurgle emitted from the owl's throat. Was it a chuckle?

"I hear whispers on the wind and voices in the night. There are few in this valley that have not heard your name and the legend of the river of fire. You stopped the death."

Now it was Raven's turn to chuckle.

"Bilgat said we were creating legends. What else do they say?"

"Well, let's see. There's a new leaf-frog story. He wouldn't have lived much longer you know, he was an old frog. A dying Mother Goose legend, and some banter about a ring-necked gull with a short life span. I've even heard some rumours that involve Great Eagle, but that's about where I stopped listening to all that nonsense. That old bird died years ago. Besides, it was getting too ridiculous, to say the least, especially when they started rambling on about you wearing the clothes of man ... as if they would fit." She chuckled again as she eyed up Raven.

"You know you'd look really silly wearing those human foot wraps and I just can't imagine how you could get your wings into one of those upper-appendage coverings. Hoo Hoo." By now the owl was shaking all over, as her imagination expanded on such a good joke. "Then there was the bit where you were swallowed up by a man-made machine and carried off, never to be seen again. HOOO HOOO HOOO HOO. I'm sorry but it's really hilarious."

She gurgled and shook, tears coming to her eyes blinding her to the scowl that formed on Raven's face.

"It's just as I thought," she gurgled away, "obviously the stories were greatly exaggerated. Here you are in my tree, not lying dead in the stomach of a metallic monster and I certainly don't see anything but feathers on your back. Pity," she did her best to get control of herself, "the stories were quite entertaining, even if they were unbelievable."

She raised a wing across her eyes, wiping away the tears of mirth, and sat shaking with uncontrollable glee.

Raven held back the urge to transform himself right there on the spot. The evening breeze that filtered through the branches gently pulled at his feathers, reminding him where he was. A quick glance down was enough to stifle his indignation and the desire to prove himself. He was too high in the tree and there was no room for a human body to squeeze between these branches, that's if the change in weight didn't snap the branch and send him tumbling.

The thought of a human form being stuck like a cat at the top of this mighty cedar tweaked Raven's funny feather. His indignation at the owl's rejection of his deeds dissolved. Let's face it, even he would have had trouble believing the stories if he hadn't actually lived through them. He didn't look any different than he had those many months ago before that fateful trip up the river with the frog.

'River of fire' that was a good one, Raven thought, it had certainly burned the frog. If he hadn't saved it with that maple leaf, maybe none of the rest would have happened. Strange how one small act could cause such a huge ripple effect.

Well maybe he didn't look any different but, if he was really honest with himself, he felt different inside. Begrudgingly, he had to agree with the owl's assessment. It was all too incredible and, in today's world of man, totally unbelievable.

Unless you believed in the spirits that is.

Few did these days.

But he did.

Now.

He knew that, after all these years, the spirits had returned.

"Well you're wrong on one count at least, the great eagle isn't dead."

The owl looked annoyed. "Well he should be. Father has flown over him countless times. I can't understand it. Maybe you are mistaken and he's a figment of your imagination, I hear you've got a really good one. Must have, if you create things like they say you do." The sarcasm dripped from her beak.

"No, I assure you he was flesh and feather and in fine form when I left. Besides, I don't create things, I change them."

"Ooh hoooo, so it WAS your doing. Nearly dead was he, when you saw him, full of rhumatail and arthriticks, down to his last gasp and counting? Father must be losing his touch. I can see I'll have to check up on him more often. If a job needs doing these days seems you have to do it yourself if you want it done properly." She scowled at the raven. "Changed him back into a spring chick I suppose?"

Greatly exaggerated but too close to the truth for comfort. Raven scowled back, sleep was fighting a battle with his brain. He had let her rant, but her voice was no longer soothing; it had sharpened and was becoming extremely irritating.

"Madam, I have no idea what you're talking about. He was very much alive. Old, tired maybe, but far from dead. All I did was straighten a few bones. He's certainly no 'spring chick'."

"Ohoo, Madam is it now. What would you know? Death is inevitable; it's the freeing of the mind and the releasing of the body. It's a lousy job but someone's got to do it."

On the other branch, the owl was not tired in the slightest. The night was young and she was in fine fighting form. Raven shook his head as a wave of sleep swept over him.

"Unless the spirit isn't ready to leave."

"What are you talking about? What have the spirits got to do with it?"

He realized that effort would be needed to convert the owl, and, at this time of night, he doubted he would sound very convincing. As if they had a will of their own, his eyes closed.

His silence was all the owl needed. With a small snort, ah, there was that hint of disrespect that Raven was more used to, the owl shuffled to a clear spot on her branch.

"Well I can see if there's any spirits around here they're all in your head. It's obvious you're not going to be sociable, so I'm off. With any luck that damned eagle has left me some dinner."

That said, she spread her wings and headed out, through the branches, into the night.

Raven's eyes flew open.

"Eagle? Did you say 'eagle'? WHAT EAGLE?"

Raven's words were lost in the rush of air from Owl's powerful wings. She was gone.

"Night owls, night hawks, damn them all." Raven muttered as he re-fluffed his feathers and resettled into his mossy perch, determined to get some sleep before the morning chorus started.

5
The Beach

Far to the north, a mist crept over the sea. Dawn was spreading along the horizon and the sky grew lighter.

As the early morning light stretched across the seascape, the mist thickened and congealed into a dense fog. It blocked out the rising sun, absorbing what light was left, turning everything a sickly, silver gray.

Wisps slid in stealthy fingers across the surface of the ocean where they reached a small raft that drifted with the tide, and enveloped it.

On that raft White Raven woke to a damp chill creeping under his feathers, causing his very bones to ache. At first he wondered where he was, it was so much like the mornings he had woken up to for so many years. Then, as he raised his head, he felt his movement ripple through the raft, and he remembered.

HE WAS FREE!

Free from that spirit-forsaken island. His glee became subdued as he looked into the dense shroud surrounding his craft. The water was calm at least but with a fog like this, it was going to be impossible to figure out where he was. It was so thick he couldn't even gauge the direction of the sun. So, was he still heading south or was he being carried west and further away from the shore? Which way to flap? He had no clue. The stillness was ominous. He ached all over and only his empty rumbling stomach broke the silence. He hadn't accounted for the weather, and had expected to be within sight of land by now. He should have brought some food with him, poor planning on his part. He frowned at the water as it slid under and past the raft. Never having mastered the art of fishing, he scowled at a few bits of seaweed as they drifted toward him and, when they floated alongside, he pecked at them half-heartedly.

Yuck, to think that ducks ate this garbage.

Hours passed and the fog, unbelievably, thickened. It seemed to have a mind of it's own and was attracted to his raft and trying to block his escape. Little drops of water suspended in mid air, that's all, no mind, no body, just dense fog: nothing sinister about it. White Raven still shivered.

Tendrils licked up and over the bundle of balls, and the dampness saturated the raven's feathers. His stomach gave up rumbling. The few scraps of weed from the ocean had stopped the complaints. Starvation was preferable to the salt-laden, half rotten offerings drifting by. For the first time ever, White Raven wished for a storm, a wind, a breeze, anything to lift this dirty grey blanket.

White Raven had never experienced fear; it was not in his make-up. Instead his years of pent up anger and frustration surfaced. He forgot about the time he had found himself trapped on the island, when his screaming at the wind and rain went un-answered. He had forgotten. He screeched, then he screeched again and again.

No one answered.

More hours passed and a very despondent, wet mop of dingy white feathers began eyeing up the floating debris again. He was about to check out what looked like a plastic bag when he heard a distant sound. He turned his head, concentrating on not causing the balls to creak as they rubbed together. Sure enough, there it was again, a low, ghostly moan muffled by the fog. He held his breath, waiting until it came again, then again. Each time it was a little clearer. Minutes passed and it grew louder: from which direction was confusing. He counted the seconds till the deathly silence was broken again by the ominous sound.

Ooo-aaah

As the time passed the sound grew louder and louder. Was some animal wailing in the fog?

OOO-AAAH . . . OOH-AAAH.

The haunting call drifted across the water, piercing the band of fog, shredding the silence, throwing it out over the vast sea.

A worried White Raven studied the ripples, gauging the drift of the current. Was it his imagination or was he moving faster? A piece of driftwood floated past and every now and then, small whirlpools appeared, but as quickly as they came, they vanished. Another clump of

---

weed. Yes, he was definitely speeding up and the ocean had begun to undulate.

The wind began to rise thinning out the fog and, through it, he could make out a towering shape, the source of the OOO-AAAHs that were now deafening. The sound resonated in his skull, grinding it's way into the core of his soul. The shape became more distinct, its lines more defined. A tower above jagged rocks. Was some monster trapped inside screaming out in pain?

The swell began to make life uncomfortable as well as threatening to break-up his workmanship. The wind tore at his feathers. His muscles still ached from last nights escape. He was too weak to fly. His stomach lurched as he scrambled to re-twist several knots that were threatening to unravel when, in between the blasting OOO and the moaning AAAH, he heard another very familiar sound.

A very unpleasant sound.

A sound that could spell disaster if you were at the mercy of the sea, which unfortunately, he was.

The crashing sound of breaking waves.

Through the mist White Raven caught a glimpse of ominous, black cliffs. The tower, with its jagged rocks, was now behind him but the water had begun churning and swirling in all directions and, as his craft spun in circles, the raven had to grip hard to prevent himself from being tossed into a sea gone mad. The water seemed to have absorbed all the pent up anger from the white raven and was now throwing it all back at him. Troughs between the waves grew deeper, the foam, a filthy yellow, and back eddies boiled.

The pounding waves tore at the rocks, so loud they drowned out the moaning tower as they greeted their next target, a small white raven.

The violence of the wind tore the tops off the waves, throwing sprays of icy cold water over the raft. Over his shoulder, White Raven saw a huge wall of water coming towards him. It grew higher and higher, towering above the little raft. It curled, and the last thing the white raven saw was a great sheet of foam as water crashed down on him. He gripped one of the knots in the tangle of ropes and for the first time in his whole life he called upon the spirits

As the white raven was dragged down into the dark depths of the ocean, the ozone layer high above the storm rippled: his call was heard.

Perched on top of the black cliffs was an old eagle. It was mid-morning and every day since his mate had left he had flown to this spot and sat looking out over the ocean. He could still picture her, soaring out over the waves, a routine flight, yet she never returned. Although beyond her egg bearing years, she was still majestic and he missed her.

He spotted the glass balls first. Scattered along the beach wedged in with other bits of tidal junk, the sun glinting off the glass, he was surprised to count so many. He hadn't seen glass floats like these for many years and to see so many all at once was unexpected. Nowadays, fishermen used plastic or cork floats.

His old eyes searched, taking their time studying each ball and the surrounding pieces of driftwood along the entire length of beach. A gull worked its way along the tide line, occasionally stopping to peck at this and that. Eventually the eagle spotted a bedraggled clump of white feathers. A cold chill ran up his spine, old stories and ancient legends, his mind groped with distant memories of tales told by his grandfather.

* * *

The story of a white raven who fought with an eagle came to mind. The raven in that story was from another time and had strong spiritual powers. The legend told how the thieving raven decided to steal eggs from an eagle's nest. However when he arrived at the nest he found the eggs had hatched. Gleefully he picked up the largest eaglet in his talons and was about to bite off it's head when the mother eagle returned. A great fight ensued, during which the raven hung onto the fledgling. Only when the male eagle flew in to help his mate did he drop the small bird. The youngster fell through the branches but was lucky and survived. The mother bird managed to pick him up and return him to the nest. Apart from a few bruises the only other damage was a bad scrape across the top of his head. He was over a year old before the adult feathers finally grew in covering the scars. They were pure white as a reminder to all eagles to protect their young from the evil of the white raven.

* * *

As the old eagle struggled to recall the details of the legend, he watched the gull approach the sodden clump.

White Raven's mind drifted. He could hear the surf as it thundered and crashed on the beach, he could feel the warm sun on his back, and he could feel a pressure holding him down. Strangely enough he felt safe, as if he was back in his egg. The warmth on his back reminded him of his mother. He snuggled deeper, his mind floating free from his body, content at last.

Peck.

Pain stabbed him in the head.

Peck. Peck.

A sharp beak attacked his skull and all his senses rushed back in self-defense.

Peck.

"Cr-a-a-o-ck." White Raven spat sand out of his beak. His salt encrusted eyes flew open and looked into the startled face of a large herring gull. As White Raven tried to lift his head, he realized he was half buried in the sand, and the effort sent the gull screeching into the air.

The gull landed a short distance away on a large piece of driftwood, reluctant to give up what had looked like a very promising meal. From this safe perch the terrified gull watched as his early morning breakfast struggled, lifting first one wing then the other out of the grip of the wet sand. Bits of debris clung to sodden feathers and, as White Raven rose from the grips of his sandy grave, the gull sat transfixed by the horrendous sight.

The sand rose in the shape of a giant bird. It had the beak of a raven, but it wasn't black, it was a dirty, scummy yellow. Seaweed, streaming from its back, added to the effect of a monstrous creature from the deep. When the evil looking, bloodshot, beady eyes swung in his direction, and the whole apparition suddenly lurched toward him, the seagull quickly decided he wasn't that hungry, and fled in terror.

The sun beat down unmercifully. With sand and weeds still clinging to his feathers, White Raven struggled to get his waterlogged body up the beach, away from the incoming tide. He was battered, his strength drained, and, as his senses reluctantly returned to his head, so did a pounding headache. Every square inch of his body was bruised and patches of his feathers were missing. His remaining tail feathers were twisted in their sockets and over half of his pinions were torn completely from his wing. Flying was out of the question, survival meant finding some shade, resting and trying to conserve what little strength he had left.

Higher up the beach, the fine sand turned to gravel then, finally, round smooth pebbles interspersed with larger rocks. It was a slow, exhausting and excruciatingly painful trek up that short stretch of burning hot sand but finally, the not-so-white raven collapsed in the shade of a large chunk of granite and closed his eyes.

It was well into the afternoon before he woke. The sun had crept around the rock and found his head again. The sleep had done him good, at least now he could lift his head without feeling that it was going to explode. He opened his eyes cautiously; the encrusted salt and sand scratching at his eyeballs. Easing his body back into the last of the remaining shade, he surveyed his surroundings.

The incoming tide was now receding and the indents he had left in the sand had washed away. There was a massive expanse of sand glistening in the sun. A heat haze distorted the view of the ocean and he couldn't look in that direction for long without the glare burning his pupils. He turned his head and studied the rest of the beach. It curved, forming a shallow bay. At one end, the black cliff rose sharply but the rest of the beach, as far as his eyes could see, was edged with a staggering array of old weather-beaten logs. Behind the vast array of wood sand dunes rose, covered with sea-grass and scrubby wind-bent pines.

It was a wild, windswept and deserted beach, rugged and unforgiving, but to White Raven it looked like the Promised Land. Well maybe not exactly as promised, but at least it wasn't that forsaken island. He was on the mainland, he knew it, things felt different somehow and, no matter what his eyes told him, he had the feeling he was not alone.

Down the beach the hull of an old shipwreck lay partly submerged in the sand. It was close to the tide line and covered with rust and green weed. A starfish hung from one of the portholes and barnacles clung to the planking.

White Raven needed food. Not only was the side of the wreck covered in crustaceans but it looked as if there were clumps of muscles hanging amongst the seaweed. Muscles had softer shells than clams and were usually easy to crush. They would make a good meal.

The raven pulled himself upright, made a sad attempt at shaking off the last of the sand from his feathers, flexed his bruised muscles, and proceeded to hop across the sand to the wreck. He moved with as big a hops as he could but it still seemed an eternity before he was in the cool shade of the old timbers.

The movement of the tide had carved out a hollow where the hull sank into the beach and created a pool of seawater. A movement in the water caught White Raven's eye. The pool was home to a number of small creatures and a young rock crab was trying to scramble out of sight. White Raven's beak moved fast and the moist flesh of the crab quenched his parched throat as he swallowed. He overturned a few rocks at the edge of the pool and was rewarded with a feast of immature crabs and sand fleas. They were soon followed by mussels. As he had suspected, the underside of the planking was covered in great clumps of the shellfish that clung to the old timbers. For a long time the only sound that could be heard above the distant crashing of the waves was the crunch of shells.

The sun was much lower in the sky when he finally sat back satisfied, his stomach no longer complaining. He raised a stiff and battered wing, trying to straighten a few of his remaining flight feathers. They would heal in time, but damn if he wanted to sit on this beach forever. He was a mess. Bits of seaweed still clung in the hardest to reach places and his coat was covered in dried dirty scum. He needed a bath, but preferably not a salt water one, he'd had enough salt water to last him a lifetime. He eyed the tidal pool, and, with resignation, decided it would have to do. At least it looked clean and would probably get off the last of the weeds although he doubted it would do much for the scum.

He scowled at his reflection. He couldn't remember when he had last tasted water that wasn't mixed with salt. Even the rain on the island was brackish. During storms, waves would throw up huge clouds of spray tainting all the water reserves on that blasted rock.

White Raven sighed. Deep within his soul he wished it was a fresh mountain stream, how he missed the taste of pure, clean water.

He looked across the beach, to the sand dunes and beyond. Tomorrow he would tackle that journey and maybe he would find a nice pond or creek but, for now, he looked back at the pool. Maybe if he closed his eyes he could pretend it was a clear freshwater spring. He scowled again, yes, he said to himself again, it would have to do, no good wishing for things you can't have. It sparkled, inviting and, with a deep sigh, the raven stepped in.

In the shadow of the old boat hull, the water was surprisingly cool and refreshing. It eased the burning in his aching muscles and he felt the tension from the last two days seep out through his feathers.

"Aaahh."

He knew he was exhausted yet it seemed incredible that salt water could feel this invigorating.

A small crab floated to the top of the water, then another, followed by several sand hoppers. They struggled in a weak attempt to reach the edge of the pool. His eyes were drawn to the water's edge; it was alive with a mass exodus of critters.

"What the . . .?"

The water felt so good, his brain at first refused to focus on anything but the pleasure of the moment. It struggled, but curiosity won.

What on earth had caused the creatures to leave the protection of their rocky homes in the water?

Surely not him? He'd never seen anything like it before.

Another crab floated close to his beak. Out of curiosity he pecked at it. It was almost dead and had no strength left to escape his prying beak. He really wasn't hungry any more but when tasty little morsels are delivered right to your beak. Well, why waste good food? He delicately picked up the crab, tossed his head and crunched down.

"Yech."

He spat it out with such a force it flew across the pool and stuck to the side of the wreck. Something was definitely wrong with the taste of that crab. The thought of poison crossed his mind, it had tasted bland, had absolutely no flavour and the seafood salty taste had gone.

That's what was missing, salt. It no longer tasted salty. White Raven's eyes grew wide, if they grew any wider they would pop out of his head. His beak hung suspended from his jaw as his thoughts raced. He looked down at the water.

"How on earth . . . ?"

Very slowly, as if he was afraid of startling something, he dipped his beak into the pool and cautiously tasted it with his tongue. Incredible, it tasted like a fresh mountain stream, clean, clear and pure, no wonder the crabs had all left in such a hurry.

The raven tentatively took a very small sip. Then another. Nothing else had changed; he was just sitting in a nice clear pool of mountain water instead of a salty tidal one. No big deal, it wasn't poisoned. Maybe in the buffeting of the waves his brain had addled. Or, maybe it was just his imagination playing tricks on him, he had heard of things like that happening when you were out in the sun too long. Who knows how long he had lain trapped in the sand with the sun beating a tattoo on his head. That must be it; wishful thinking had turned a normal salty tidal pool into a fresh water spring. He'd wake up soon and find it was just one of those nasty little tricks that dreams play on you when you're not feeling your best.

He took another sip.

Normal, salty, tidal pool, my claw.

The battering of his brain over the last few days

hadn't slowed down his thinking process. The water must have been salty or there would have been no crabs. The only thing that could have changed the water was the presence of a raven. When he stepped into the pool, maybe he had disturbed an underwater spring. A bit more thought and he discarded that idea, the water had no trace of salt in it and an underwater spring in the middle of a tidal pool would be brackish.

He squinted up at the towering hulk above him, certainly no help there, no fresh water coming from that direction. He tasted the water again, still having a hard time believing. It was still fresh and as clear as the minute he had stepped into it. He shook his head, a very puzzled frown creased his forehead and caused his feathers to twist in a confused direction. The water was too clear, his once filthy feathers looked sparking white under the surface. He lifted a wing. It was no illusion, his feathers were the cleanest he had seen them in a very long time. The scum had vanished; there was no trace of it. It had magically disappeared.

His mind, struggling with the reality of the situation, grabbed at the new idea. A magic pool, why not? He'd heard of wishing wells. His power of reason sat back and relaxed, finally feeling it had some semblance of control. Salt water into fresh, hmmm, pretty neat trick. If only he had mastered that one during those miserable months of isolation, at least he could have had a decent bath.

As reluctantly as he had entered the pool, he eventually stepped out and shook himself, feeling a hundred eggs better. Even his flight feathers looked less battered and he could see the start of pinfeathers already growing to replace the broken ones. That pool must have healing powers too.

Well, why not? If it was magic, it would have. Wouldn't it?

He looked back at his reflection, silhouetted by the setting sun, and smirked. He felt like a different bird. Things were definitely looking up.

Or down, depending on your point of view.

What did you go and do that for? First you save him from the deep, now this.
I dunno, it is HIS brother is it not? Besides he called us.
So he may have, but he is the banished one.
He has been screaming at us for years, now he has escaped.
Trouble, that is what I call it. Trouble.

Hovering high above, in the ever-thinning layers of the ozone, the same two spirits watched. Watching is what spirits do best.

It's hard to describe a spirit when there's nothing visual to describe. Greed, generosity, revulsion, compassion, and all the other usual love, hate stuff are the life forces that fuel the spirits. Some are good; some are bad. That's life. But, in the spirit world there is no such thing as good or bad, emotions are emotions, without them you're dead. I mean really dead. No more of anything, nothing, nada, zip, abort, delete, and certainly no retry or ignore.

Which is why, at the general meeting of minds back in the year after a catastrophic world war, there was a unanimous decision by the upper echelon of the high council, to keep the greed and hate down to small-scale disturbances. Larger ones tended to erupt into violence which snuffs out life, a lot of lives actually, too many for comfort. The old spirits were strong on comfort. No life, no emotions, no replenishing of the spirits. Call it survival tactics, but keeping the balance was the ultimate goal, with the odds stacked on peace and quiet. Contact with the world of the flesh was restricted to very special cases. Ones least likely to cause trouble. Spirits were trained from their very conception to watch.

Yes, watching is what spirits do best.

The high council will not like it.
Who is going to tell them?

The tone said it all; looks don't count when you can't see them.

Besides, if they were that concerned, why did they put old Spfzztzzch! on watch duty over such a remote outstation? He has never managed to stay in one place for more than a decade. Any small disturbance and he has to check it out. Just walks off his job, totally irresponsible, I say. Now look what has happened. The raven has escaped.

Below, White Raven continued preening his feathers.

If there is good and bad in everybody, as fate dictates, then such a gift should inspire the good, right?
Not in this case, he is a bird of a different feather, and I do not mean the fact that he is white.
But you said they came from the same egg.
Yes, an egg that was secretly touched by the high council.
Really. What was so secret?
I do not know, it was a secret.
Oh reeeally!

With renewed interest the spirits returned to watching as the sun finally sank beneath the waves. White birds are easy to see, even in dark shadows. It seemed feathers require a lot of preening.

The spirits weren't the only ones watching. The old eagle still sat on his lofty perch. Age may have slowed him a little, but after some heavy thinking, the old legends had slowly started to surface and the more he remembered, the more he worried. Watching the crabs exit from the pool and the white raven drinking what should have been salt water was almost enough but, when the raven finally left the pool a transformed bird, he knew his suspicions were correct, and, if the rest of the legends of the white raven were true, there was going to be trouble.

Just the same, I still think we should inform the council.
Why? This is interesting.
Well . . .
It could be our secret. We have our own special raven to watch.
Hmmm . . .

The idea was neither bad nor good. It was just an idea. It had merit. Reporting the escape would undoubtedly cause a major disturbance.

Peace and quiet, that was the mandate. So peace and quiet it would be. The spiritual presence nodded, not visually of course, just more bouncing of the airwaves. As far as the high council was concerned, ignorance would be bliss, . . . or so these spirits thought.

6
The Call

Back in the valley, Raven woke late. The sun was well above the tree tops and there was no sign of the owl.

Pity, he thought, I might have gotten some idea in which direction to look for Bilgat. He stretched his wing muscles and peered out through the branches. The surface of the lake was flat calm with hardly a ripple on the water. The winds in the bay must have blown themselves out. The gulls were gone from the beach and there was no sign of Bilgat, or any other eagle for that matter.

The crayfish had made a nice supper but it was a meal that required a lot of work. Maybe, if the storm

---

had settled down for the day, he could find an easier breakfast down by the old mill landing.

There was a light breeze, out-flowing from the upper reaches of the valley. It was warm and gentle on his back as he flew down the river to the estuary and the deserted mill site. He circled and landed on a haphazard collection of logs. The log float had originally been anchored and used for tying up log booms and boom-boats. Now, abandoned by the mill, the logs were slowly rotting away. The cables wrapped around them, holding them together, had rusted through in places. Small plants, grasses and even trees, had taken root in the decaying wood. It resembled a small island. Healthy green weed floated on the surface of the water and Raven hopped along the boom looking for debris caught between the cracks. You never knew what tasty morsel you might find trapped.

A nice collection of mussels hung from a half submerged cable at one end of the float. Some had already grown to quite a size, much larger than they were a few months ago, and with a little effort they would make a tasty meal. His strong beak tore off one of the larger shellfish. It came away easily and with a quick flick of his head he smashed it against the tangle of cables. It shattered and, with a grunt of pleasure, Raven hooked out the juicy meat, swallowing it whole.

It's almost too easy, he thought, as he worked his way along the cables, tearing off only the largest shells, leaving the smaller ones for another day. The light breeze kept the usual pesky flies from joining him at his breakfast table. The sun peeked out from behind puffy white clouds. Altogether, it was a very pleasant morning; almost too pleasant. It was enough to make a raven nervous.

A large, blue heron flew across the bay toward the float, his wings beating a slow, sedate pattern. He arced down and the long legs, that had stretched out behind him when he flew, came forward. With wings half folded, the feathers spread out, acting as a windbreak. A few backward flaps, claws grip the nearest log, the long appendages fold and, with a few more flaps for balance, the heron landed.

Raven nodded his head toward his visitor.

"Morning Captain," he croaked, "had breakfast yet?"

With a flick of his beak he tossed a large mussel in the general direction of the heron.

Captain Blue eyed up the raven thoughtfully, before he deftly flicked the muscle out of its shell.

"Had a late night, did you?" He remarked. "Check the sun, it's almost mid-day."

"Well then join me for lunch. A female owl kept me awake half the night. I've no idea how dark it was when I finally got some shuteye, damned bird has a fixation about death."

"You must have been up at the lake. Sounds like you met one of Call-my-Name's daughters. Probably Spirit-Flies or Last-Call. The locals have a saying regarding that family. By the way, did she fly in over your head?" A small amount of concern crept into the heron's voice.

"No, I don't think so. It seems I chose to roost in her favourite tree. One minute I was alone, the next minute she was there, just as I was dozing off. Then, when she left, she flew down underneath my branch. Why?"

"Oh don't worry about it, just a silly rumour."

"Well if it's anything like the rest of the silly rumours going around the valley, I won't."

Deep in the heron's throat a chuckle gurgled.

"Thanks for the mussel. Actually, this end of the float is a good spot for perch. They like to hide under the logs, in the shade where the ends are wedged up into the bank."

As if to demonstrate he dipped his head in the water and, with a quick twist of his long neck, a small fish landed on the log in front of the raven. It was a beautiful blue and yellow striped sea perch.

Raven's eyes lit up. "Haven't seen one of those for a long time, thanks."

"Well I have to say, fishing has been much better this winter since you cleaned up the river. I can't remember when it was this good."

Raven fluffed up his feathers. There weren't many birds left in the bay that didn't know about Raven's new-found abilities, thanks to the squawking of the loudmouthed gulls, but most had stayed their distance, watching him from the treetops with suspicious eyes. Only the old heron, Captain Blue, and Bilgat, the young eagle, had helped him with the change. He valued their friendship and advice. Certainly none of the other residents of the bay had given him any thanks for his efforts, or credit for the improvement in their lives. Not that he expected much, but some respect might be a good start.

"Well your advice helped," he said with the grace that comes from knowing the praise was well deserved. "It set me on the right track."

Captain Blue nodded his head, acknowledging the statement but, being one to not waste movement, as his head dipped it suddenly dropped and in a flash another perch was struggling in his beak. A quick twist of the heron's head, a swallow, and the unfortunate fish flapped its way down the dark turbulent stream that led to the great sea beyond.

"So, now that the river is clean, what are you going do?" Captain Blue asked the one question most parents ask of their young when they have completed their learning. If the question had come from anyone else

Raven would probably have spat out some smart-aleck retort. But for some unearthly reason the raven listened to the heron, almost as if he were a distant relative, an elder. Ridiculous really as, apart from the fact they both had feathers and a beak, it was impossible to find any similarity between the two bird species. All the same, the feeling was there, deep beneath his feathers; respect.

* * *

Legend tells us that it was the Heron who helped raise Raven's great, great grandfather and, when they parted, gave him the gift of a coat of feathers, enabling him to fly.

* * *

"Dunno," mumbled Raven shrugging his wings. "Life seems a bit dull at the moment."

He idly flicked a few of the empty mussel shells back into the water.

"Don't see the need for a transformer around here any more," he muttered. "Everything seems fine just the way it is."

The heron gave him a quizzical look.

"This bay is a very small part of the ocean, the valley is a very small slice of the island. Life may seem better here but there are lots of other bays and valleys plus a whole world full of problems. You know, there is a saying that if you're looking for trouble, it will come to you. So I don't think you'll be bored for long. You might want to make the most of it, take the weight off your feathers and relax a bit."

Raven flinched. He was bored but he didn't realize his actions had made it that obvious.

High up on the top of a nearby rocky ridge, Bilgat sat listening. Many months had passed since he left the protection of his home in the distant inlet that wound deep within the mountainous mainland. He had crossed the waters of the strait to come to this bay, the home of Raven. He had watched as Raven gathered his courage to use his newfound skills and put them to good use. He had stood by as awareness of his friend's abilities had slowly sunk in and Raven had come to terms with them. He watched and waited, hoping against hope that the raven would not turn to the ways of his forefathers and become a thief and a trickster. His own great, great grandfather had warned him that boredom is one of the first signs that mischief may occur.

Not that he was sure of what he would do if the raven did turn down the wrong flight path, so he just sat and watched, and listened, and worried.

The afternoon breeze was replaced by a cool wind from the north. It reminded him of his home back in the mountains. His feathers perked up a bit as he caught the tail end of the heron's speech. His ability to mind read, an inherent trait in all bald eagles on the west coast, had helped a lot when giving Raven advice. It also allowed him to get some idea of what Raven was planning.

The breeze shifted and an up-draft pulled at Bilgat's pinions. He lazily stretched his wings and, with little effort, lifted off the ridge and let the wind carry him. He circled higher and higher, the valley spread out beneath him as far as he could see. He drifted from one up-draft to the next, trying vainly to put his concerns behind him, when his senses caught a distant call. It surprised him enough that he misjudged the next up-draft and plummeted a few feet before he managed to get himself back in control. He flapped as quickly as possible, regaining altitude, then circled in a glide, ears straining to catch the message again.

He was surprised, because eagles had stopped sending messages over long distances. Surprised, because, these days, long distance messages tended to get scrambled and mixed up with shrill ringing sounds that pierced the ear, odd little musical jingles, and the high-pitched voices of people. Humans had somehow found a way to send messages through the air, like voices on the wind. At first it had upset and confused the eagles and they had begun to wonder if they were losing their minds. None of the messages had made any sense; there were questions without answers and answers when there were no questions. Then Bilgat had seen the little boxes that humans carried in their pockets and now knew, and understood, that it was these little human-made pieces of plastic that had caused the problem.

The voice that came to him now sounded far away. It was different from the human voices and had the tone of an elder. Not only was the call shaky but the words were spoken in rhyme, just like the old story tellers used to do.

"North by flight . . . A Raven White . . . escaped by night   . . . the spir . . . gone
. . . . . . wrong . . . change is near . . . trouble . . . fear"

"The spirits? The spirits what? Gone, gone where? A white raven, escaped? Change, what will change?"

Bilgat strained to hear more, but the wind was silent.

"White raven, what white raven?"

Bilgat waited but there was nothing. The wind had shifted again. He sent out a call but distant sending was not something he was good at. It was a lost art. When he tried again an eagle roosting across the bay called back at him.

"Afternoon Bilgat, what's got your feathers in a twist?"

"Did you hear that distant call that came over the air just a few minutes ago?" He replied. "It sounded really strange."

"Sorry, wasn't listening. The wife's been complaining that the nest's not big enough. It's been fine for the last three years, but you know how it is. All I heard was your call. I can check down the valley for you if you want. If it was important, I'm sure someone else will have heard it."

"Thanks, I'll check back with you later, all the best to your wife and eggs."

Bilgat turned his head back into the wind. Now it was coming from the northwest. From this height he could see the ridge of mountains that were the backbone of this great island. There was still a heavy coating of snow on the peaks, clouds scudded along the ridge and hung up on the highest crags.

How far north? He wondered. Over those mountains?

The wind had shifted back yet again but there were still no more calls, not even a whisper, it did however carry the unmistakable scent of snow. The call may or may not have come from the other side of the range but the wind certainly had. Perhaps one of the eagles at the head of the lake had heard the call. It hadn't sounded like a cry for help, more of a warning really.

I wonder what Raven will make of it, thought Bilgat as his eyes went back to the small log float. He could just make out a tiny black speck. The raven was still there. He raised his head and filled his lungs with the cool mountain air, stretched his wings, turned his head into the wind and flew down and out over the water. As he flew across the bay, a warm up-draft teased his feathers and he circled in a graceful glide back toward the raven and Captain Blue.

His smooth wide-claw landing was destroyed as he staggered, hopping clumsily to one side, trying to avoid the mess on the float. Much to his disgust he lost his balance and ended up sitting in the middle of the pile of broken mussel shells.

"I could have cut my talons to shreds." He scowled at the culprit, who, after hopping quickly out of the way, now watched, with what suspiciously looked like a glint of amusement in his eyes, while the eagle picked bits of shell from his tail feathers.

"Gulls would have cleaned up after we left." Raven answered defensively. "Besides, with lots of other logs to choose from, you really didn't have to aim for that one. Can't say it was one of your better landings."

Bilgat glared at his friend . . . well more of an associate really, a comrade in flight. He sighed, admitting to himself that the message had distracted him enough that he had not paid heed to his landing site. Raven wasn't a bad bird, but it was obvious that lack of direction was irritating him and in turn he was starting to take pleasure in the discomfort of others.

"I came to tell you, I need to take a trip up the valley," he snapped, "and I don't know how long I'll be gone."

Raven stiffened, his whole attention now focused on the small eagle.

"Why?" He croaked, blunt and to the point as usual.

The feathers above Bilgat's eyes flattened as he thought carefully before he answered.

"I don't really know for sure, but I just caught part of a very odd message coming from the direction of the mountains. It sounded like a warning. It might even have come from the other side."

Raven snorted in disgust. "Gi'mme a break, that's nearly two or three days flight from here. Your family is only two days away and you can't hear them. So what makes you so sure it's not from just up the lake?"

"I can't be sure, but the wind was cool at the time with the scent of snow. I could almost taste it. The message was weak and it sounded as though it came from a very old bird. If it came from someone at the lake it would have been clearer, besides the eagles at the lake don't talk in riddles."

"Riddles? What do you mean 'Riddles'?"

"Riddles, you know a sort of rhyme. This message

was like an old chant, a song, it rhymed."

Now it was Raven's turn to look puzzled, but before he could ask the next rather obvious question, Captain Blue spoke. He had listened to the conversation closely and although birds of prey, eagles in particular, made him nervous, this one was smaller than most; less of a threat.

"May I be so bold as to ask the nature of the message?"

"Yeah," said Raven, "just what I was about to ask."

The eagle looked long and hard at the heron. He recalled Raven's story about the advice the old fellow had given him during his struggle to understand the strange things that were happening to him.

Well why not, he thought. Who knows, he is an elder, he might understand the message, it wouldn't hurt to pass it by him.

Bilgat repeated the message as best he could with the appropriate gaps.

He looked at the Captain, who slowly shook his head, then at Raven.

"That's it?"

"Ahuh."

"Well, I don't like the sound of that. Especially the last word."

Raven hesitated, frowning as he groped with a rather unpleasant memory. One he had tried hard to forget.

"Funny, I had a brother once. He was white. He was also mean. I wasn't sad to see the back of him. Left kinda sudden, and I haven't seen or heard of him since."

"Interesting," said Bilgat, "it sounds as though this raven was trapped or something, and escaped. It also sounds as though someone doesn't want him loose."

"Well if it was my brother, then I'm inclined to agree with whoever sent the message. He was trouble."

Bilgat nodded. "I sent a call to the eagle across the bay. Unfortunately he was busy at the time and didn't hear the strange message."

"More preoccupied with that young wife of his, I bet," sniggered Raven.

"Be that as it may, he said he'd check with the eagles at the head of the lake but I think I'll take a trip and ask them myself.

"North by flight." Captain Blue repeated the first words of the message. "If you need to go over those mountains, you'll have to go west first, to the deep inlet. It would be a tough flight, even then. Those peaks are pretty high and it's extremely cold up there, even in the summer. I seem to recall a narrow valley that cuts through the worst of them that might make the flight easier. I believe the trumpeter swans use it every year as part of their migration route. They are late leaving this year because of the storms but they will go soon. If you decide to head north, you could follow them."

Raven shuddered, between Canada geese and trumpeter swans he wasn't sure which were worse. The trumpeters were larger, more aggressive, and every fall, around the middle of November, a flock of three hundred or more arrived in the valley. They would cover the fields and marshes, their honking going on long after dark. Noisy and aggressive, give him a mute swan any day. At least they didn't keep you awake at night.

"At a safe distance, I hope," he muttered. "Shouldn't be too hard. They stand out clearly against the mountains and we'd be able to hear them from miles away."

"Pardon?" said Bilgat. "What's with the 'we'? You don't have to come. I'm the only one who heard the call. It might be nothing."

Raven fluffed his feathers and looked hurt.

"I thought we were a team. Your grandfather thought you could help me, that we could help each other. We did a good job cleaning up the river. I reckon I should come along. Besides, if it is my brother, you'll need my help."

Bilgat looked down at his talons.

"Sorry Raven," he said. "I guess I didn't think you would want to bother flying halfway across the island following nothing more than a whisper on the wind."

"Well you thought wrong. If you think it's important enough to fly up the valley, then I'm coming too, and that's final."

7
Recovery

To the north, a cool, early morning breeze woke White Raven. The tide, that had been out most of the night, was on its way in again, creeping up the beach and bringing the breeze with it. He had slept well, all things considered. It was now time to leave the shelter of the old wreck before the tide reached it and the sun started heating up the sand. Besides he was starting to feel peckish again, he'd eaten all the mussels and the crabs had all left the pool. His eyes returned to the calm water. It was still clear and sparkled in the early morning light.

He hated to leave it but couldn't live on water alone.

'Maybe not' he decided 'but I can, at least, take some of it with me.'

He forced his stiff muscles into action and hopped over to the pool, dipped his beak into the cool water and took a long drink. As the refreshing liquid ran down his throat, he studied the beach. It could be some time before he found another water supply. His wings were useless, no matter how clean the feathers looked, flying was out of the question. With so many feathers missing or damaged, the most he could manage was a pathetic flap that barely lifted him off the ground.

An idea popped into his head.

Maybe this magic pool was a wishing well . . . in which case . . . well . . . why not? There was no harm in trying. He looked again at his battered wing, held his breath and turned back to the pool.

"I wish my feathers were healed so I can fly again."

NO.!!!! Don't you DARE. You do and I WILL report you. OK. OK. You do not have to rattle the airwaves. It was just wishful thinking, there was no power in it, he has no conviction, no beliefs, no control.

YET

White Raven scowled at the water. Nothing. His feathers were still twisted and bent. He snorted in disgust at his own naivety. Whatever had changed the water last night, it certainly wasn't granting wishes this morning. Sullen, he turned away and, without looking back, headed up the beach toward the distant barricade of logs and the sand dunes beyond.

It was a wide beach, typical of the west coast. The logs, piled during the winter storms, were further away than they originally seemed, especially when you are used to judging distance in wing beats. Bruised legs and broken claws certainly don't help. Jagged pieces of shell and barnacles buried in the sand cut into the white raven's feet. Every time he staggered or fell, a rock found another sore muscle to twist. By the time he reached the jumble of driftwood, he was exhausted and collapsed in the hollow of a large, weather-beaten cedar root. He lay there aching but exhilarated. He'd made it across the open stretch. At least now he was well out of the reach of the waves.

After a short rest, he hauled himself up and worked his way around the cedar stump. Over, under and between the logs he stumbled. They were piled haphazardly into a maze and working his way through them, especially when ground bound, was time consuming. The logs at the back were rotten from age but offered a late breakfast of wood bugs, beetles and centipedes which replenished some of his strength.

Apart from the occasional gull flying overhead, White Raven hadn't seen any other sign of life all morning. As he struggled over the last log and clambered to the top of a grass-covered sand dune, he spotted an eagle high in the sky. It was circling, barely a dot against the cloud bank that was coming in from the north.

From the top of the dune he could also see a band of trees in the far distance. Real live trees, not the scrubby half dead things that had clung to that pitiful lump of rock that called itself an island. Pine, Cedar, Douglas-fir, oh, how he had missed the smell of pine needles. With renewed resolve he hopped and fluttered his way down the far side of the sand hill and up the next.

The weather, as unpredictable as usual, had changed and, by midday heavy clouds were rolling in. At least the sun wasn't pounding on his head, but the wind was rising and the dunes were becoming increasingly unpleasant. Sand blew off the tops of the mounds and was whipped into whirling clouds in the gullies. The wind found ways to force grains under his feathers, grinding his flesh like sandpaper, scraping at his already raw wounds. Was the whole world against him? He wondered if the eyes had discovered his escape and the spirits were now putting every obstacle they could find in his way. The sand scratched his eyes, almost blinding him, causing him to stumble into a scrubby little pine. Anger and resentment swelled in his chest again. Driven by the pain penetrating to the very shafts of his feathers, he struggled to the top of the next hillock, turned his head into the wind and screeched his anger. His whole body was in torment. He willed the wind to turn back, demanding that it stop, screeching at the top of his voice he commanded it to leave him alone.

The wind died.

The swirling sand dropped back.

The only sound was the thunder of the waves as they crashed down on the beach behind him.

Now you HAVE done it, I warned you.

No I did not.

What do you mean, No you did not. I just saw you.

Well you are wrong for once. This time I did nothing.

You must have.

No I did not, I tell you, I thought you did it.

The air thickened

Uh Oh

What do you mean Uh Oh?

Will you quit that. If you did not do it and I did not do it then who?

Well I guess there is only one explanation. There is only one other being that could have done it.

Who?

Him.

What do you mean, him . . .?

Oh for love of man, you fool. He did it himself.

He has the potential to harness the power. They both do.

Now that we have removed the barriers between our realm and theirs. Now he has used it.

Once he realizes he has the power to change things we will be in for trouble. Mark my words.

I knew it, we should have reported his escape.

White Raven stood ramrod straight on top of the sand dune. He tingled all over and his tail feathers twitched. His senses felt numb and his reasoning was so completely scrambled, it took several minutes to recognize any sensible thoughts.

Lightning, I've been struck by lightning.

No, there was no flash.

Earthquake?

The ground didn't move.

The wind, what stopped the wind?

His mind raced through all the reasonable possibilities, none of them fit. His brain, still struggling to put things in some semblance of order, finally decided there was nothing left except the unreasonable.

I told it to stop, and it stopped, he thought.

The answer seemed so incredible that it had to be true. Besides it was the only answer left, even if it didn't make any sense.

He had stopped the wind.

Well, if that was the case, had he changed the water

too? Possibly he had, but if so, then why couldn't he fly?

Maybe you can.

That inner voice sounded sooo reasonable.

Well, wishing it hadn't worked. Something must have been different. He looked across the remaining dunes; it was still a long hop. The trees didn't look any closer than they had five sand dunes ago.

"I wish I could fly," he shouted out loud. Then again, louder. "I want to fly."

The scream died and the waves continued to crash on the shore behind him. The wind, which had turned back on itself, was struggling to regain control, racing round and round in circles stirring up a sandstorm at the far end of the beach.

No change.

White Raven flapped his wings. Nothing, still no lift. Even though you would think it impossible, his feathers looked even worse. The pool may have removed some of the scum and weed, but the wind had covered him with so much dust and sand that it stuck to the damp feathers turning him back into a badly carved sand sculpture.

His mounting anger so confused his befuddled brain it threw out one last desperate idea, the spirits were watching and were playing tricks on him.

"Damn you," he screamed up at the turbulent sky. "Damn you all. You think you're so clever. Well I'll show you. You'll see. I can fly and you can't stop me."

He flapped his wings again, anger driving each down beat. Harder and harder, he beat the air and, with an almost insane screech, he leapt off the top of the dune. His twisted pinions straightened, his tail feathers filled out and he soared into the sky.

8
Through the Mountains

Bilgat and Raven flew side-by-side back to the lake.
As soon as they were within sight of the calm
waters, Bilgat sent out a call to the local eagles, but
none had heard the unusual message. Not stopping to
rest, the two birds flew on.

The lake was several miles long, one of the largest on
the island, so more than an hour passed before the two
birds neared the head of it. Mist that clung to the tops
of the surrounding mountains crept lower the further
inland they flew. By the time they reached the far shore,

the two birds were flying through a steady drizzle of rain.

Several small streams along the shoreline fed into the lake. The largest, at the head of the valley, was turbulent at this time of year. Although a small gentle stream in the summer, cutting it's way through the mountains, in winter it put on a different face, roaring into the lake carrying soil, rocks and even uprooted trees. The surrounding lake water, being full of silt, was not very deep and Bilgat soon spotted a small trout that had wandered into the shallows.

"I suppose you're hungry again." He looked askance at the raven.

"Always." Raven grinned, as he too spotted the fish and watched his friend drop, talons extended, scoop the fish effortlessly, then land on a gravel beach.

There was a delicious head waiting for him when he landed on the shore. Bilgat hardly responded to Raven's thanks, his head cocked to one side as though listening.

"Anything?"

Bilgat shrugged.

"Nothing, there are several eyries at the head of this valley, but no one heard a thing. It's possible that now we're too close to the mountains and the call was blocked. I was flying high when I heard it and calls have been known to 'bounce'."

Raven shook his head, not really understanding the technical details of the air and sound waves. It was all as confusing as a tangle of seaweed to him.

"So now what?" He asked.

"We follow the trumpeters through the mountains."

Bilgat looked across the water at a flock of swans gathered on the mud flats, as he spoke.

"They will be leaving soon, and, by the sounds of it, making an early start tomorrow morning."

"I'm surprised you can make any sense out of that racket, and I thought geese were bad. I'm beginning to think I might have been wrong. They honk right through the night you know, we'll never get any sleep, unless . . ." A mischievous look came into his eyes and before Bilgat could stop him there was silence.

"You can't do that." Bilgat cried.

"Too late," Raven snickered, "I just did. Oh don't fluff your feathers. I didn't change them. I changed us, you and me, I created selective hearing."

Bilgat snorted, slightly mollified. "That's nothing new, all birds have selective hearing, especially my father."

Raven frowned.

"That's not what I meant and you know it. I just tuned out the honking of the swans. I included you in the equation but . . . if you prefer . . ."

"No, no . . . I was just giving you a bad time. If you didn't alter the swans then I reckon that's OK. Although, maybe you should put a time limit on your little trick or we won't hear them leave in the morning. I wouldn't want to wake and find them gone."

Raven was getting used to Bilgat always questioning his tricks. Trouble was, he had to admit the eagle was usually right.

"I guess," he relented, studying the swans carefully. "Now you mention it they do seem a bit agitated. You don't think they'll leave in the middle of the night do you?"

"The last I heard, before you tuned them out, was that they were taking to wing at first light. The yearlings need daylight to learn the migatory flight path. Also there is another group yet to arrive and they are agitated because they are already a day late. Lucky for us as the group from the south were probably delayed by that storm."

Relenting a little as he saw the worried look in the raven's eyes, he added, "Don't worry, I think we can relax for a few hours, get some rest. I suspect it will be a long flight tomorrow."

The raven and the eagle finished their meal in silence. The only sounds they could hear came from the gentle slap of the waves on the beach and the murmur of the wind as it wove through the trees behind them.

Slowly savouring his last mouthful, Raven looked around eyeing up the trees along the shoreline, looking for a comfortable roost. A large, first growth Douglas-fir caught his eye. It stood out, tall above the surrounding forest. During the early logging days, loggers left a big tree close to the water's edge to be used as a crane.

Called a Spar tree, pulley and tackle were attached to the top of it. Logs cut from the surrounding forest were then dragged by ropes or chains to the water. There they were rolled down the bank to form rafts or log booms to be towed away by tugs. The spar tree was often left standing for possible future use. This one looked very old and, although all it's lower limbs were trimmed those many years ago, the top had continued to grow, making it an excellent roost for birds that preferred tall trees.

Bilgat nodded. "I already chose that one, if you don't mind, I'll take the top branch."

Knowing that Bilgat could read his thoughts, Raven didn't bother to reply out loud.

You're welcome. Personally I find treetops a bit drafty. I'll take a lower limb closer to the level of the rest of the forest.

They had barely settled on their respective branches when Bilgat spotted the last group of swans flying in formation, silhouetted against the dark green of the valley slopes. As they neared the end of their long flight, they flew lower, their white wings reflected in the still, almost black, water of the lake. They circled in a wide sweeping arc, flying right over the top of the tall fir and swooping down to land on the lake not far from the rest of the flock. The whole mass of swans along the shoreline rose up, stretching necks, and flapping wings in a bizarre dance of welcome.

"It has come to mind that I didn't thank you," Bilgat's sleepy voice drifted down through the branches. "I suspect that the welcome we just witnessed was deafening."

Raven smirked. "Nice to know I'm appreciated. I still can't figure out when those birds get any sleep, unless they're deaf to their own racket."

"I told you selective hearing was nothing new." Then, as an after thought, Bilgat added with a yawn, "maybe it's a lullaby in swan."

Raven chuckled. "A swan song? That's good that is. Never in a million years would you be able to make a song out of all that honking."

He settled down on his branch. It was too early in the spring for crickets and even the frogs were silent. The evening breeze had died and, apart from the occasional distant hoot of an owl, all was quiet as the light faded into the darkness of the night.

It seemed Raven had only just closed his eyes when the honking started. He shook off the grips of sleep and opened one eye. An early morning mist was rising from the lake enshrouding them in a blanket. They could hear the swans but it was impossible to see them. He could barely distinguish the end of the branch.

"It sounds as though they're leaving."

Bilgat appeared out of the fog and landed just in front of Raven.

"Can't see a thing in this mist. It will be hard to see which stream they follow. There are two that head toward the mountains. We can only hope we choose the right one and that the mist clears as we get away from the water."

Raven hated mist and fog; it was clammy and cold. He had changed a lot of things over the last few months but weather wasn't one of them. He had to do something or they would lose sight of the swans. They were on the move and getting further and further away. He could hear their honks but they were definitely growing fainter. If he and Bilgat chose the wrong valley it could be a hard crossing. His mind raced through the options.

"Get ready." He yelled at Bilgat, and launched himself into a sudden torrential downpour of rain.

The mist vanished.

Through the curtain of water they could just see the tail end of the last few swans as they flew over the treetops toward a towering cliff of rock.

"Cute trick," gasped Bilgat as they raced to catch up.

"Just increased the diameter of the water drops. Sorry, hard to judge size. Didn't mean to create such a deluge."

"Hey, it worked, don't worry about it." Bilgat's voice turned from assertive to puzzlement as his eyes followed the last of the swans.

"But where on earth are those swans going? The rest of the flock have vanished. They're not following either of the streams. It's a good job you cleared that mist as I certainly wouldn't have thought to fly in this direction."

Ahead of them, the last of the swans vanished. As the two companions neared the face of the cliff, they saw there was a very narrow canyon cut into the rocky ridge that was almost completely hidden by the trees. It was so narrow that, in places, trees had fallen across the gap and wedged in the opposite wall creating bridges. It zigged and zagged through the mountains turning north, then west, then north again.

Occasionally a distant honk echoed back to them letting them know they were still on the right track, which was good because the swans were now so far ahead that, because of the twists and turns in the canyon, they were nowhere in sight.

At one point the canyon closed in so tight it seemed there was not enough room for an eagle to fly through let alone accommodate the width of a swan's wingspan.

"They must fly through in single file," commented Bilgat, trying not to let claustrophobia affect his flying skills.

Then, quite unexpectedly, as they rounded another curve, the canyon widened enough for them to fly side by side again. The walls fell away and they could see they were now deep in heart of the mountains, the tops of which were still covered with snow. The rain had stopped just after they had entered the gorge; now the air was decidedly chill as they climbed higher with each turn.

On and on they flew.

"Don't they stop for a rest?" Grumbled Raven. "We didn't even have breakfast and it must be getting close to midday."

The continuous weaving back and forth through the gullies was taking it's toll. Even Bilgat, who was more used to soaring and high level flying, was tiring.

"It can't be much further, I think the honks are getting louder. They must have stopped."

The words were hardly out of his beak when they rounded the next corner and there, stretched out before them, was a pristine mountain lake. The snow from the top of the surrounding peaks came right down to the narrow shoreline, now crowded with the trumpeter swans.

Bilgat looked over his shoulder at the cliff face. They were well above the tree line but the canyon opening was as obscure from here as it was hidden at the other end, little more than a chip in the rocks.

"I can see several ledges up there on the bluff at the end of the canyon. It's probably our best hope for a good rest, unless you want to join the swans on the beach."

Raven was too tired to answer the intended sarcasm. In unison the two turned back, flying up to land on a comfortable looking ledge with a convenient overhang.

"At least we should stay dry if it decides to rain again," said Bilgat making a feeble attempt to be cheerful.

Raven grunted, as he folded his aching wings. Every muscle in his back, right down to his tail feathers were screaming in agony. It was much worse now that they had stopped flying, the pinion pain was excruciating.

"I feel as old as your grandfather," he muttered as he hopped to the back of the ledge, away from the cold up draft that rose from the valley floor. "I need some hot rocks warmed by the sun, and a good meal."

Bilgat, thanks to his early morning exercise routines, was already recovering from the long flight. He stood on the edge of the ledge looking down on the huge flock. It

---

seemed the swans were settling down for the rest of the afternoon and were in no hurry to depart. They huddled in small family groups along the shoreline feeding from the shallows and preening their feathers. The excited honking was beginning to calm down and he could catch the occasional one that made sense. An early morning flight was being planned again for tomorrow; the rest of the day would allow the cygnets to recuperate.

Thank goodness for that, he thought. Then, turning to the, now dozing, raven he said. "I can't do much about the 'hot rocks', but I will check out that lake for 'a good meal'."

Leaving Raven to wallow in his sorrows, Bilgat flew out over the small lake in search for food.

It wasn't long before his sharp eyes spotted a shadow moving just beneath the surface of the water. A local resident, not used to all the commotion in its waters, had come to the surface to see what was going on. Bilgat dropped quickly and his talons plucked the unlucky fish from his home, the afternoon sun reflecting off it's scales in a rainbow of colours.

Almost too pretty to eat, he thought, as he flew back to join Raven on their lofty ledge. Almost.

9
Fish . . .

He was flying.
Actually flying. With each down beat of his wings White Raven felt himself getting stronger. The trees that had seemed so far away when he was on the ground, now passed quickly beneath him as he flew inland. He didn't care in which direction he headed, his one purpose over so many years was to escape, and escape he had. His mind had so long been fixated on breaking free from the spiritual force surrounding the forsaken islet that any further thoughts had just been wishful dreaming. He had no plan, no specific flight path and

for nearly two hours he just flew, reveling in his new found strength and freedom.

Eventually his stomach regained some semblance of control and managed to get its message through the euphoria in his brain. Food was needed to fuel a body that was bent on such vigorous exercise. Loath to come back down to earth, White Raven did his best to ignore the demands, but, eventually, nature had its way and he gave in. Scanning the treetops ahead he spotted an opening and, as he flew closer, he could see a cut in the forest caused by a gravel road. It looked well used and he decided to follow it. Roads often led to human habitation. Humans were wasteful. Where there were humans, there was garbage. Where there was garbage, there was an easy meal. White Raven liked easy.

He followed the road as it twisted and wound through the mountains, calming his appetite with the promise of a meal at the end of it. The valley widened and the road came to an end. In front of him was a long narrow harbour. Clustered around the end of the main road were a small number of houses, all facing the water. They were rather weather beaten but on the inland side of the road there were larger buildings and what looked like a general store. At first glance it was hard to tell if the water of the basin was the ocean or a lake, the sides of the mountain, on the far side of the inlet, were so steep that the trees reflected dark green in the placid waters. A small wharf, lined with ocean-going fishing boats, was the only clue that this protected cove, cut deep into the backbone of the island, fed into the sea.

White Raven circled the buildings then landed in a tall fir. Having flown for a good part of the day he was tired but took his time studying the little village. He mapped out the different side streets, most of which lead to houses or barns. He was assessing the chances that the road leading up the hill was the most likely route to the village dump when, from the corner of his eye, he saw movement down at the docks. One of the boats looked as if it was unloading its catch.

FISH.

His stomach lurched in anticipation. It couldn't remember when it had last processed fresh fish.

There was the usual cluster of frantic gulls clamouring around the boat, a good sign that a meal was in the offing. Leaving the fir tree, White Raven flew across the docks, spiraling down through the very centre of the flock, which scattered in alarm, and landed on the wharf directly behind the boat. A quick glance told him that the gulls had already eaten everything thrown overboard. Was he too late? Seeing two men working on the trawler, he decided to get closer. He flew up and landed on the stern of the boat. The men were packing fish into a large container and covering them with ice. Already there were two such containers stacked on the dock, probably waiting for a human to collect them and take them to some distant city full of people. The sight of all that fish made the raven feel quite faint. With caution he stepped nearer.

The men were used to the sight and sound of the screaming gulls, they were part of the scenery around any fishing boat with a hold full of fish. It was several minutes before one of them spotted the white raven perched on the railing of the boat.

"Hey, Al, look what we have here."

Al, who was busy cleaning out the last few remaining fish from the bottom of the hold, took several minutes to respond.

"What?" His head finally looked up. He squinted at the bird perched on the side of the boat.

"Cheeky blighter." His hand reached behind him, searching for something to fling at the invading bird.

"Oh for Pete's sake, Al, put your glasses on. It ain't a damn seagull."

"Huh?" Al groped in his shirt pocket and pulled out a pair of battered looking spectacles. Hooking them over his ears he peered, near sighted, at the apparition before him.

"Good Lord." He gasped in astonishment as his eyes finally came into focus. "A bloody white raven. I've never seen one of them before. Where the hell did he come from?"

"Dunno, but he looks mighty hungry to me. Chuck him the head off one of those damaged fish."

Al reached into an old bucket tucked in the back corner of the deck and pulled out a fairly large fish. It had an ugly gash in it's side from being caught in the netting. The men usually kept such fish for their own consumption or gave them away to friends. The bruising of the flesh made it unsalable but there was a lot of good edible meat left. Taking a knife from a tray beside him, Al sliced off the head and tossed it across the deck.

White Raven didn't hesitate; he flew down and greedily attacked the head. The men watched in fascination.

"Here, Wilf, you reckon he's an omen?"

"I'm not sayin' it is or isn't, though I hope it's a good one. I don't recall any record of a white raven in these parts, ever."

"Sam up in the village might know. His grandfather was pretty high up the totem pole in the local native band. We should talk to him."

"Yeah, fishin's not been bad lately but those poor blighters that work for the mill could do with some luck about now. Another bunch will be laid off by the end of the week."

They continued to watch as the white raven finished

---

the last scrap of flesh from the head of the fish.

"Don't think I've ever seen a fish skull picked so clean or so quickly in my whole life. I reckon he was real hungry. Chuck him the rest of that fish, Al, we got plenty this time."

Al reached into the bucket, pulled out the decapitated fish and threw it across the deck to join the remains of it's head.

White Raven couldn't believe his fortune. His black beady eyes studied the two men standing watching him. Was it a trick? A trap of some kind? Maybe a plot to capture him. He hesitated. His stomach growled, the smell of the freshly cut fish gnawed at his insides. He threw caution to the wind, hopped forward, and attacked the fish as the men watched in dumbfounded amazement. A fish almost the size of the bird slowly vanished as chunk after chunk disappeared into that huge beak.

White Raven ate, and ate and ate, till the fish was nothing but bone. His beak was covered in scales and his chest feathers were smeared with blood. His stomach strained, working as fast as it could to process the harvest, packing the protein into every square inch of storage space it could find. Finally there was no more room and, if he ate another mouthful, the raven knew his guts would throw it back out. Then, and only then, did the white raven stop eating.

"Would you believe it?" Al took off his glasses and proceeded to clean them with a rather grubby rag, as if cleaning them would change the fact that the bird had eaten almost the entire fish.

"There was enough fish there to feed an entire family. Where the hell did he put it all?"

Wilf had his head to one side studying the raven with a puzzled look on his face.

"You know, Al, I think he's doubled in size. He

---

weren't much bigger than one of them seagulls till we fed him. Just look at the size of him now."

White Raven stretched his neck in an attempt to clean the bits from his feathers, at the same time he started backing away from the near proximity of the two men. In his greed he had hopped quite close, now his senses cautioned him to put as much space between himself and the remains of this unexpected feast as possible.

Al dropped his voice to almost a whisper. "Grab that end of the net, Wilf." His own hand was already reaching out to the netting on the deck beside him.

Too late, almost as if reading their minds, White Raven's acute sense of self-preservation took flight and, with a leap, spreading of wings, and a mighty flap, he was gone. Over the side of the boat he flew, skimming across the surface of the dark waters, heading toward the trees on the far side of the inlet.

The two men stood side by side on the boat, watching, as he vanished into the trees.

High above, riding the thermals to stay aloft without flapping his wings and expending any more energy than necessary, soared the old eagle. He had sent out several messages this morning but received no replies. Tonight and early tomorrow he would try again. The mountains surrounding this inlet were higher than where he was before; maybe someone would hear his call. The local birds just ignored him these days. He was getting old and they put his concerns down to flights of his imagination. His feathers were dry and his talons cracked, but his eyesight and mind were still sharp.

Trouble was getting stronger by the minute and there was very little an old eagle like him could do except watch and wait, hoping someone would respond to his warnings.

The spirits watched too. Even the silence felt guilty.

10
Fried Feathers.

The fact that it was the beginning of April didn't mean
much to either Raven or Bilgat, but ice crusting the
edges of the lake when they woke did. The trumpeters
didn't sound impressed either; their deep honking
echoed around the valley.

"Have you noticed they honk loudest at takeoff and
landing?" Bilgat remarked, as he fluffed up his feathers
against the early morning chill, making him seem larger
than he really was.

"Oh no, not again. There goes our chance to have
some breakfast. Now I know what they have under all
those feathers, a stomach large enough to hold a week's
supply of food."

The words were barely out of Raven's mouth when the first swan started its noisy flap and splatter across the water in it's preparation for takeoff. Within minutes, the stillness of the morning air was broken by the honking of nearly three hundred trumpeter swans as they followed their leader across the lake and into the sky. Rising into the airspace above the lake, they spread out like a massive, white flying carpet. In unison, they flew once around the valley, slowly and sedately gaining height as the last straggler joined the flock which eventually turned north.

Raven let out a deep sigh.

"I never believe in too much exercise on an empty stomach." He grumbled. "It puts air in your gut and confuses your next meal into thinking it's gone the wrong way when you swallow it. Comes right back up again. Nasty. I had indigestion all last night because of yesterday."

Bilgat chuckled as he started to prepare for takeoff.

"It was your friend's idea to follow the swans."

"Was it? I must have been daft to listen. As if these little wings of mine thought they could keep up with a swan. Where was my head at?"

Bilgat stepped back from the cliff edge, tipping his head as he listened to Raven's grumbling. Balancing on one leg, he lifted his other claw and started methodically cleaning his talons.

"It's you're call." He said. "We can turn back now and be back at the lake in time for supper."

"Yeah we could," and, with a snarl that rivaled any bear, the raven took to the sky, heading north, following the mass of white wings that were beginning to blend with what looked like an early morning fog at the head of the valley.

Bilgat chuckled to himself. I guess I'd better not mention that the mist looks more like a snow flurry to me, he thought as he spread his wings and launched himself after his companion.

Raven was halfway down the valley before realizing he was starting to chill. Usually the act of flying warmed his feathers; instead he was feeling as if it were the middle of winter.

When the first cold blast hit him broadside, and snow whipped over and around his body, his frustration at being forced to fly on an empty stomach dissipated. A snow flurry; he hadn't anticipated having to deal with white stuff this late in the spring. He did his best to think warm but, with the lack of breakfast and still being half asleep, the cold had already started to numb his brain. The swans had vanished into the white swirling blizzard and Raven was losing his sense of direction. At least the stuff was dry and didn't stick to his feathers like the snow in the valley back home. If it did it could freeze his wings at this altitude, it would at least turn to ice on his feathers.

Think warm.

Trying to fluff up your feathers whilst flying through a snowstorm is futile.

Think warm.

A hot surge of warm blood pounded through his veins, his heart pumped and his skin tingled. If you could have felt under his feathers he was hot to touch, too hot.

"WARM . . . Not burning hot."

Raven opened his beak, swallowing as many snow flakes as he could in an attempt to cool down. His whole system was at boiling point and the snow was now a welcome relief. Just as he was about to plummet down in an attempt to find a snowdrift to bury himself in, the squall stopped and the two birds found themselves flying through clear skies once again. The mountains on either side of them were steep and the valley was wide. In the distance, water glistened. There was no sign of the swans.

Raven's eyes searched and Bilgat flew high, almost into the into the clouds, circling, but it looked like the swans must have taken a different valley. From the angle of the sun it was clear they were now flying west toward the coastline on the other side of the island, the mountains were behind them.

"I don't think we need the swans any more, that looks like the ocean ahead. Once we reach there I can send out another call then, hopefully, we can follow the shore line." Bilgat soared down to fly along side Raven again. "Besides I'm better at finding us a fish in the sea than back in those mountains."

The further down the valley they flew, the larger the expanse of water ahead of them became until it was obvious that the eagle was right, they were flying toward the ocean. Raven's stomach growled and the thought of food ahead added strength to his wings. Just the same, it was many wing beats later before they were flying over an estuary that led into a wide inlet. Raven was numb; all feeling had gone from his wings. They just beat automatically and his body felt as if it was being stretched out over hot jagged rocks, stung by thousands of mosquitoes, then left to dry like seaweed at low tide.

"That don't look like fresh water," he gasped, "I'm parched and I need a drink."

"I'm not surprised, you got so hot back there I could see steam rising off your back. OK, OK, I'm sorry."

The words going through Raven's head were unprintable, his scowl was threatening. Bilgat knew when to keep his beak shut.

"Look." He pointed his beak at the far shore. "I can see a small stream running down the rock face. It's just ahead; only a few more wing beats."

Bilgat circled into the incoming breeze. Raven followed, although from this height, he couldn't see the stream, still he trusted the eagle's excellent eyesight.

The rocky cliff face was broken up with large patches of green moss clinging to narrow ledges on the gray-white granite walls. Small fir and cedar trees grew out of every conceivable crack, although it seemed impossible that even one tree could find the nourishment it needed to grow on this towering wall. Tumbling over the top of the cliff, a small, fast-flowing, creek splashed its way down to the dark waters of the inlet. Bilgat landed on an outcrop of rock just behind the top of the ridge where the water had formed a small pool. Raven didn't waste any time, he flew right in and splash-landed in the middle of the pool. Spreading his wings, letting the cool mountain water flow over his feathers, he let out a huge sigh of pleasure as his skin cooled.

The eagle studied the raven as he submerged himself in the pool and tried very hard not to let amusement creep into his voice

"You know, I think you singed your tail feathers, they're looking a bit brown."

Then, glancing at his own beautiful, pure white tail, he added. "And I'm really glad you didn't try that trick on me."

"Just a slight miscalculation." Raven retorted, not wanting to admit that he had very nearly cooked himself. Then, as his body slowly gained some feeling of relief, a suspicious thought popped into his head.

"You could have warned me," he snapped, "I'm damn sure you saw that snow flurry long before I flew into it. Come to think of it, where were you? Flying above it I suppose."

Bilgat, pretending not to hear, was intently studying the base of the cliff.

"Sorry Raven," he said "but I think I see lunch down there and I reckon we could both do with a good meal. You cool off, I'll be back in a few minutes."

"You're avoiding the subject," Raven yelled as the eagle took flight. "Subject . . . subject . . . subject." His words echoed around the inlet.

"Blasted bird, I could swear that sounded more like a chuckle." His indignation over the possibility that the eagle had avoided the snow was mixed with anticipation of relieving his grumbling stomach. He stepped out of the pool and craned his neck, inspecting his feathers. His tail did look a bit off colour with brown scorched patches at the tip.

Hmmm, I'll think twice before I try that one again, he thought, as he tweaked a few stray feathers back into place. Cute trick though. With a bit of practice things could be a lot more comfortable during those long cold winter nights. Maybe if I just work on increasing my down feathers or warming the air at the base of the quills.

His thoughts were interrupted by the sharp, high pitched call of the eagle. Peering down from the cliff top, Raven saw he had indeed caught a fish; lunch as promised. A couple of gulls had also spotted the eagle's catch and were circling, hoping to steal a bite. When Raven flew down to join his companion, the gulls stopped their clamouring. For almost half a minute their wings franticly beat the air, beaks hung open and their eyes almost popped out of their heads. Just seconds really, then the gulls turned and fled down the inlet towards the open waters.

"It seems your reputation has spread this far." Bilgat flicked the fish head across the rock to the raven. "Our presence has just been announced. By tonight there won't be a gull on the west coast that doesn't know you're here."

"Well they'd better keep their distance or I'll mute the lot of them." Raven was beginning to feel more like his old self, and he paused between mouthfuls to take a good look at their surroundings.

The small beach was at the widest part of the inlet and across the water from them, a small grouping of rocky, tree-covered islands clustered together. The incoming water swirled and undulated with the force of the tide, making it quite choppy but, behind the islands, it was placid and looked inviting.

"Actually that's where I found the fish."

Bilgat was reading the raven's mind.

"Well, why don't we take a rest for the afternoon amongst those islands?" Raven suggested hopefully, "You can check with the local eyries and find out where we are. Who knows, maybe one of them heard that call of yours."

Bilgat nodded. At low tide the islands would also have a good supply of shellfish, crabs, and urchins; the birds certainly wouldn't go hungry.

The White Raven

11
Sunny Days and Donuts

Further north,
White Raven woke to a misty
drizzle. You know the type, clammy,
damp and miserable, unable to make up its
mind whether to rain or not. It dripped down through
the trees, slowly seeping into every crack. The clouds
were so low he couldn't see across the inlet.

Dark, dank, dismal, and dreary, no sun doth shine
and the world is weary . . . It was not the sort of day to
cheer the soul unless you were a duck.

It certainly soured the mood of the white raven as he peered through the branches of the Sitka spruce he had chosen for his night's rest. With his stomach still full from the feast of fish the day before, he planned to check out the rest of the village. If all the town's residents were as generous as the men last night, he reckoned he might stay a while. He thought back over the conversation between the two men. What was it Al had said? Something about an omen. He chuckled to himself. Small communities, especially fishing ones, were bound to be superstitious. Well, if that's what they thought, maybe he should play along with the game. First things first though, he squinted up through the tree in the direction that his senses told him the sun should be.

"Lazy sun of a . . ." he muttered.

* * *

The sun had a very poor reputation, one that went back many years to the times of the first people. His character was carved in legend, the old stories were repeated down through the centuries. He was known as a gambler, a wastrel who spent most of his nights drinking and partying. Trouble with that is, some mornings he would be either too tired, too drunk, or just too plain lazy to even bother to wake up, and most days he fell asleep on the job.

* * *

Maybe back on his island prison the spirits had some say in the weather, but here on the main island, there was no excuse for bad weather, at least not in the mind of White Raven. After years of miserable weather like this he had had enough.

"Wake up, you lazy no-good sun of a . . ." he yelled up at the clouds. "Where in the sky are you?"

Fog, which was happily drifting through the trees,

shrank back at the raven's screech.

"For pinions' sake, WAKE UP." White Raven's voice rose to a high-pitched shriek.

The fine mist shriveled up into tight balls, shrinking away from the anger. It hesitated for a few seconds, undecided, then rose out of the trees trailing wisps of vapor behind it like the tentacles of a jellyfish. Rising higher, the tendrils finally let go of the branches and blue sky began to appear. As the fog continued to rise, reforming into white puffy clouds above the mountains, a very groggy sun poked his head out from behind the highest peak, his dismal face peering through the blue patches.

He hadn't done very well at the gambling tables making for a long night. The effect from the few extra drinks he had consumed to console himself, hadn't worn off yet. He staggered across the morning sky wondering what in the universe had woken him and why he was being dragged from his bed. He finally settled just above the ridge, nursing a major hangover. The clouds were slow to disperse, quite expecting the sun to go back to sleep. He didn't, he couldn't, no matter how hard he tried. He finally gave up the struggle and scowled down at the earth, scaring away the last of the morning moisture.

"That's more like it." White Raven settled back on his branch, enjoying the warmth of the sun's rays as they penetrated the feathers on his back. Things were definitely improving, a full stomach, a warm roost, what more could a bird ask for? A little entertainment maybe?

"Hmmmm."

White Raven eyed the group of buildings across the bay. He saw movement as people went about their daily chores. People, they could be very entertaining. He studied the town for a while. There was a lot of activity about three quarters of the way down the main street.

Certainly worthy of investigation, he thought, and, with a quick glance up to make sure the sun was still alive, he took to wing, flying across the waters of the harbour toward the settlement.

He landed on the edge of the roof of what appeared to be a place of food. There certainly was a delicious smell of baking bread wafting out the open door.

A table and a couple of chairs were set on the sidewalk and a group of men were settling down to enjoy their hot drinks. One of the men placed a box in the middle of the table and opened it. It was full of strange looking white and dark brown balls. When another man reached into the box, took out a ball and bit into it, White Raven realized it was food. The same food that smelled so good. Not that he was hungry really, but it did look inviting. Food was food, and a raven never turns his back on food.

"Strange about the weather, just changin' like that. Thought we were in for a wet one." One of the men spoke, between bites of his food. "Forecast was for rain all week."

"An' you believe the weather forecast. When have they ever been right?"

"Funny you say that, cos' they usually are when they say it's goin' to rain. Although I admit I dunno what planet they're on when they say it's going to be warm and sunny." The man glanced up at the sky as he spoke and the movement of the white raven on the roof caught his attention.

"Well I'll be!! Fred, just look at that, must be the bird Al was on about last night."

The man, with his back to the raven, swung round in his chair. "Yeah, that sure looks like him, can't be many of them around. From what Al said, he ate three pounds of fish. Not sure I can believe that though, he's not big enough. Wilf said he moved pretty quick when they reached for the nets. Damn smart ravens are you know."

"He certainly isn't shy." With that the man facing the raven broke off a piece of his food and threw it out onto the pavement.

White Raven assessed the distance between the men and the small morsel.

'Not worth the effort,' he thought, maybe if he waited, more would be forthcoming. It had yesterday.

"Well, would you look at that? He's not daft. That crumb wasn't enough to feed a sparrow, he wants a whole bleedin' donut."

With a laugh Fred reached into the box, grabbed one of the soft balls and threw it on the sidewalk.

"Here, that was one of my super sourdough supremes. If you wanna feed 'im, chuck 'im one of your double chocolates. That was my last one." The man scowled into the box. "I was savin' it for me lunch."

"Oh quit yer gripin' I'll get yer another one. There see? That's what he wanted."

The white raven swooped down, landing a safe distance from the watching men. Keeping one eye on the group at the table in case they made a move toward him, he inched closer until he could reach out, and, stretching his neck as far as he could, grabbed at the donut. His beak pierced it and it stuck on the end of his bill. He shook his head and the morsel flew across the pavement into the gutter. He hopped after it and gleefully attacked, tearing it into chunks just big enough to swallow.

Interesting kind of 'nut', he thought as he swallowed the last chunk, I'd like to find the tree that came from.

He eyed up the men and the rest of the box.

"Not likely buddy, one's enough. Don't think all that sugar is good for a bird. Time for you to go find yer own breakfast." One of the men closed up the lid to the box and stood up. "Come on Fred, thanks to this change in the weather some of us 'ave got work to do. We'll have to get the boat ready."

As the rest of the men stood up from the table, White Raven flew to the rooftop and watched them gather their cups and the box with the remaining donuts.

"Damn weather, if we'd know it was goin' to be like this we could have gone out early today. Too late now. If it stays like this we'll be going out tomorrow. Wife won't be happy. It bein' Easter an' all. I told her, yer can't pass up on a change of weather, the season's short enough as it is." Fred muttered away to himself.

Ignoring the grumbling, the other man looked back, "Where you reckon he came from?" He asked.

"Dunno, never heard of one in these parts for a long time. Sam says it's a sign, eh."

"What kinda sign?"

"That's what I said, an he just shrugged. 'Things will change' is all he said. You know Sam, I honestly don't know why Al asked him, he's always so long winded. Half the time you can't make hide nor hair of sense outa what he says anyway. Somethin' about the spirits on the move. I ask yer, what's that supposed to mean?"

White Raven decided not to follow them. Instead he hung around the shop hoping to get a chance at more of the 'nuts'.

Several people came and went carrying the same type of box but no one stopped to eat them. Some came in cars, others walked. He hopped down onto the table, picking at a few of the crumbs left behind by the men. A small group of boys on their way to school spotted him and chased him into the air. He circled and with careful aim dropped a rather messy deposit on the top of the largest bully's head. As screams of disgust echoed down the street, White Raven returned to his rooftop.

Just as he was about to give up hope of getting any more treats, a woman came out of the shop with a small box that she put on the roof of her car while she hunted in her purse. It was the chance he was waiting for. White Raven struck. Launching himself from the roof he grabbed the handles on the top of the box with his strong beak and took to the sky, cackling at the scream of anger that followed him.

He didn't fly far; the box was heavier than expected. Closer to the centre of town he spotted a tall, flat roofed building. His landing was awkward, but he didn't care and it only took him seconds to rip open the box. Inside were smaller nuts, more bite size, raven size. One taste told him they were as good as the larger ball that the man had given him. Better in fact. Some were brown, others were coated in a white powder and some had little crunchy white bits stuck to them.

He ate the lot, enjoying the wide variety of flavours. He decided he liked the crunchy ones best, the white powder ones the least as they were messy and made him sneeze.

Well that was an excellent breakfast, he thought. Tasty food along with warmth from the sun; he cawed in pleasure. "Now to check out the rest of the town."

A couple of gulls sat on the edge of the roof. White Raven didn't noticed them at first, being so absorbed in his windfall, he hadn't seen them land. Even now they were unusually quiet for gulls. They just sat and stared at him with that gormless look that only a gull can have.

"Yah. Scat." He yelled, flapping his wings and taking a big hop toward them.

You didn't have to tell them twice.

They leapt into the air screaming and were gone; their voices echoing back long after they had vanished over the rooftops.

"Damn cowards," White Raven muttered as he hopped his way across to the parapet. Gulls were no fun. They scattered the minute you said 'Boo'. He peered over the edge of the roof and studied the rest of the little town. In one direction a group of kids was playing in a yard. There was a sharp whistle blast and he watched as they all filed into one of the buildings. A couple more cars drove past. Several were parked right in front of this building, doors opened and closed, people came and went, his intelligent black beady eyes followed their comings and goings.

There was a short metal shaft sticking out through the tar and gravel behind him and somewhere in the depths of the building an engine growled sending warm air out the vent. Along with the sun on his back the warmth enveloped him like a blanket and White Raven's whole body relaxed. Dreamily he settled down on his perch to watch the people.

He liked people. They were interesting, they did interesting things, but above all they were an excellent source of interesting food. In the last twelve hours he had eaten more fresh food than he had in the last five years.

Food that was clean and tasty, without bits of seaweed or sand stuck to it.

Food that wasn't salty, mouldy and half rotten.

Food with flavour.

Yes he liked it.

The only sounds coming from his stomach all morning were a few contented burps. By afternoon he had the idea of dive-bombing anybody that came out of the shop with food in their hands. He wasn't really hungry any more but it was fun. Most people threw their hands in the air, their food went flying and White Raven became very adept at catching the balls in mid flight. Traffic slowed as confused people ran out into the street to escape the attacks. A car swerved to avoid the low flying bird and hit another vehicle.

To the white raven's delight the chaos resulted in more people coming out of the buildings. More targets to scare. He was totally unaware that high above him an old eagle circled and even higher, where the air is thin and cold, the spirits drifted in and out of the ozone layer.

It is starting.

I can see that, I am not blind.

We should have reported him.

Well, we did not, so do not keep on about it.

I doubt there is much anyone could have done to stop him anyway, once he escaped. He has gotten much smarter over the years.

That eagle down there has been sending messages out all week.

I noticed, but so far no one has answered.

No but I heard a rumour among the gulls that a black raven has come through the mountains following the trumpeter swans.

Now that is interesting. Our raven do you think?

Maybe his eagle friend heard the call. Why do you not go and check?

What! And let everyone know we know something? How do I ask about something we are not supposed to know anything about? It was a secret remember. Besides, why should I miss all the watching?

Well surely the council must have heard the call by now.

You would think so, but maybe not. They do not usually listen to mortals, they have other, more important things to worry about.

Like what? No, no don t tell me, I know, it is another of those secrets.

It just so happened that another spirit had heard the call. His name was Spfzztzzch!, but most just called him Old! He was dozing when he heard the first message go out. Realizing the white raven had escaped, and that he was going to be held responsible, he had followed the old eagle and blocked the rest of the calls. The last thing he needed was the council on his back. He hung even higher, above the ozone, listening to his fellow spirits. Hope flooded through the essence of his soul. If Raven was on his way, things might sort themselves out after all; hopefully before the high council got wind of his indiscretion. He drifted south searching the valleys looking for signs of the black bird and his eagle companion. With a little help maybe Raven could stop his brother, then all his problems would be solved.

12
The Second call

The night was young, the moon
was full and I rather think there should
have been a light mist hanging in the trees. Instead
there was an incoming breeze that carried the pleasant
scent of the sea.

Both Bilgat and Raven had settled in early, hoping
to get a good rest that would put strength back into
their tired wings.

It was a little after midnight when the call came, the time some call the 'Hour of Death'. Bilgat was soaring high above the mountains, gliding from one up draft to another. Cool crisp air filled his lungs and the only sound was the rush of air as it pulled at his pinions. The call was high-pitched and blended with the wind. It sounded like another eagle, but Bilgat was alone. There wasn't another bird for miles around, the sky was his. There were no limits and the horizon vanished into the heat haze that rose from the distant ocean.

Another up-draft and the wind screamed in frustration, it really did sound like another eagle. Yes, there it was again, now it sounded tired and weak. He dropped to a lower thermal layer and waited.

Minutes passed then, clearly, he heard an eagle call, although the words were distorted . . . he stretched his neck as if to hear better and . . . almost fell off his perch.

It took him a few minutes to orient himself. He had been dreaming. He was roosting in a tall Douglas-fir on the west coast of the island with Raven and they were there because he had heard a strange distant call. A call much like the one in his dream, a call sent in the ways of the ancients, a call that bounced on the airwaves, a call in rhyme.

He straightened his feathers then turning his head he listened intently. The night wind was stirring the tree branches, causing them to rustle. Had he really heard a call or had it been part of his dream? Wide-awake now, he shook his head to clear the last wisps of sleep, and waited, all his senses alert.

**". . . I send my call
to one and all . . ."**

There it was. A chill went down Bilgat's spine and he felt his tail feathers twist as he responded.

"Who are you, sir?" Bilgat did his best to return the mind-call, not knowing the distance between him and the other eagle.

" **aaa**hhh . . ." it seemed there was a huge feeling of relief flowing over the airwaves.

Bilgat sat, patient, well versed in the ways of the elders.

> "Eagle Farcry of little fame,
> and you sir, your name?"

The voice had calmed and was not as loud.

"Eagle Bilgat, Master Crier. You called?"

"Yes, Yes," The anxiety in the voice was obvious; the words came fast as if Farcry was afraid he would lose contact with Bilgat.

> "I've called by night and called by day,
> I know you not, are you new this way?"

"We just arrived this side of the mountains yesterday. I heard your call a few moons ago, on the far side of the island. But I haven't heard it since. No other eagle has heard it either. I'm sorry it has taken us a few days to get here."

> "How very strange,
> I have the range.
> I may be old and often tire
> but I inherited my voice from my sire.
> A First Flight Eagle, Sir Clearcry . . .
> So I really don't see why . . ."

The old eagle rambled, muttering to himself. Bilgat's patience was stretched and finally he interrupted.

"Your call mentioned a white raven."

"Yes, yes, my call," the old eagle came out of his ramblings with a snap,

> "To one and all.
> A raven white, escaped alright.
> Washed ashore, tired and sore.
> Found power to heal, now starts to steal."

"Then I take it you've been watching him, and know where he can be found." Said Bilgat "Can you give me flight directions from here? We are in a small group of islands at the entrance to a inlet that cuts deep into the mountain ridge."

> "Hmm, near the Broken Group would be my guess,
> Toward the sea you must fly, west.
> Past High Cliff Light
> Fly north to Sandy Bight.
> Where the waters churn, east you turn.
> Over many islands, rocks and sands
> To cliffs steep, with water deep.
> In Valley Northwind, he's settled in.
> A narrow entrance, fly past Black Rocks
> Safe harbour found, a people's nest and docks."

"Thank you sir, we will head out at first light tomorrow."

> "We? You are many strong?
> It will take many to right this wrong."

'Well, no. There's just Raven and me. He's black and we believe he is the white raven's brother."

> "ANOTHER RAVEN. Black or White
> Two wrongs don't make a right."

"This one is different sir. He is the great, great grandson of Raven the Transformer. The spirits have returned and have gifted him with the power to change things. Just like the old days, when my own great, great grandfather flew over the land."

"Two birds, just two,
A raven black and you."

The old eagle seemed puzzled. He hesitated, then a tone of respect crept into his voice.

"There are legends told . . .
May I be so bold
to inquire your nest tree and family branch?
Are you of royal birth by chance?"

"Great Eagle is my great, great grandfather."

There was a big sigh, although whether it was of pleasure, relief, concern or worry, Bilgat couldn't say.

"Then the stories are true,
May the spirits be with you."

"If I may say so sir, I think they already are."

There was a deep feeling of a chuckle, as the old eagle digested Bilgat's last remark.

"Well, maybe now I can get some rest.
The last few days have been trying at best.
For the few hours left, I wish you good night,
and an offshore breeze for tomorrow's flight."

"Thank you sir, for all your efforts. We will do our best and I wish you a nice long and restful sleep."
As his mind cleared, Bilgat realized the clouds had

moved in and covered the moon. Without the stars twinkling in the sky, the night seemed ominous.

The wind had died and the silence was foreboding. Feels like the calm before a storm, he thought as he hunched down, trying to shake off the oppressive mood. He shivered. Fluffing his feathers he trapped and re-circulate his body heat, his anxiety dissipated. Maybe it was all a bad dream, after all what eagle would call in the middle of the night?

A desperate eagle, that's who. Bilgat thought. One determined to get his message out. Well, then there's the question of why no one else has heard the calls. Why, even though listening, he had heard nothing. Not a single scrap of a message since that first frantic call almost three moons ago.

Was it only three moons? It seemed much longer. Well, maybe the wind was blowing in the wrong direction, or maybe something else had blocked the calls, or . . . someone. Did the white raven have that much power?

"I hope not," he said out loud, doing his best to banish the idea.

The stillness of the night was unsettling. High above, the old spirit relaxed a little, relieved that the message had finally gotten to the right person. Relieved that if no one else had heard the old eagle's first call, maybe it would all sort itself out before . . . no he wasn't going to think about the consequences.

Bilgat tried to return to his dream of flying above the coastal range, but the feeling of freedom evaded him. What would Raven think of it all? He looked across the beach to the old cedar.

No point in us both having a sleepless night, he

thought as he ruffled up a few more feathers and, like an old brooding hen, settled down to await the dawn.

When Bilgat woke for the second time that morning, a wind had risen and the stiff, off-shore breeze carried a rather unpleasant odour.

"Well that's a first. About time you woke up. I was beginning to think you weren't going to raise a feather before noon." It was obvious that Raven was rather proud of himself as he rambled on. "I'm starving and I brought you breakfast. I've been waiting ages for you to wake up. You have no idea how hard it was not to eat it all."

There, between them, draped over a branch was the rather smelly, mangled and rotting carcass of a rabbit, recognizable only by the ears that were still intact.

"There's a road just over the ridge and I spotted a couple of buzzards circling. I managed to scare them off before they had a chance to eat all the best bits," He began tearing at the hindquarters, identifiable only by the fact it was the opposite end to the ears, and wistfully added, "they did get the eyes though."

Bilgat tried hard not to shudder. Raised in the wilderness far from man, he was used to eating fresh food and hadn't acquired the taste for animals killed on the road, especially ones that had started to deteriorate. It looked revolting and he found the smell sickening.

Oblivious to the eagle's discomfort, the raven continued tearing at the meat and finally tore off the hind section, which he promptly tossed in the direction of the still sleepy Bilgat.

"There," he said with satisfaction, "tuck in. I haven't had rabbit for ages and this one has aged to perfection. I was really lucky, another hour and there would have been nothing left. Fantastic. Such luck," and without looking up he plunged his head into the body cavity and breathed a huge sigh of bliss.

"Oh man, oh man, just look at this."

Bilgat groaned.

"Oh sorry," Raven's head withdrew from the dark and delicious depths of the rabbit.

"Can I offer you a maggot? They've just hatched and are incredibly sweet and juicy. Say are you OK? You don't look so good."

"Sleepless night, and I'm not really hungry."

Raven swallowed his mouth full of maggots and stared at the eagle. Stretching his neck, he looked Bilgat in the eyes and demanded,

"You don't have a stiff neck do you, or a chill? You do look peaked."

"No, I'm just tired, like I said, a restless night. I'll be OK after a quick flight to stretch my wings. You go ahead and enjoy your breakfast. It looks great by the way."

"Want me to save you some?"

Bilgat forced himself to look at the unrecognizable, mangled mess of skin and bone. Raven meant well and, after all, it was the first time he had provided them both with a meal.

"Maybe I'll take this thigh with me so you don't eat

it all," he bantered as cheerfully as he could, doing his best to sound enthusiastic.

"I won't be long," he snatched at the hind leg laying on the branch in front of him, spread his wings and took off into the wind.

"When I get back I'll tell you about the call that disturbed my sleep."

"What? What call?" Raven tried not to choke as he gulped down a mouthful of intestines. Finally, with his beak clear, he screeched at the departing tail feathers of the eagle as they vanished over the treetops.

"I wish you wouldn't do that." He stomped his claws down on the branch so hard it nearly dislodged the remains of the carcass.

"Damn him," the raven's eyes went back to the rabbit. All the pleasure had gone from the meal. As he gorged down the remains, his mind was no longer paying attention to flavour and texture; instead it replayed Bilgat's last words, 'the call that disturbed my sleep'. Finally, here was news and Bilgat had gone off to stretch his feathers on the wind as if it was nothing of importance.

"Damn bird," he muttered over and over again; snapping at the meat till there was nothing left of the rabbit but bone.

As soon as Bilgat was out of Raven's sight he dropped the rotten, maggot infested, chunk of meat and dove to the water's edge. He took his time wiping his talons on a mat of seaweed and had to scrub them on the sandy beach before he felt clean again. He inhaled deep breaths of fresh salt air to replace the lingering stench. Feeling better, he looked at the sky and realized he had slept away most of the morning. The sun was already high above the mountains. He'd promised the elder that they would leave at first light. Hopefully the old bird was fast asleep and would never know that he had overslept, after such an important call.

Looking back toward the stand of fir, he hoped Raven had cleaned up the rabbit. He really didn't think he could stand another close encounter with Raven's offering. He waited, counting the ripples in the water as they made their way into shore.

. . . 99, 100. Finished or not here I come, he thought and took off, heading back to the waiting raven.

Circling above the tall fir tree, catching a strong up draft he called down to Raven.

"The winds are perfect, I think we should get going. I will tell you my news on the way."

"Going? Going where?" Raven flew up to join him. "And what's all this about a message in the middle of the night? I can't believe you took flight without telling me. You really know how to spoil a good meal, you really do."

"I'm sorry Raven but I really wasn't feeling very well, and I didn't want the information to spoil your breakfast."

Slightly mollified Raven looked with concern toward his friend.

"You're not coming down with the bird flue are you? That's nasty, and if you're not careful it will kill you."

"No I'm fine, probably just lack of sleep." And to stop any more questions he quickly added, "It was the old eagle again. His name is Farcry and he's been following the white raven for several days. Watched him gathering strength. Even though the raven was apparently washed ashore in bad shape, he has managed to heal himself quickly, almost too quickly. He's settled in at a village not far up the coast from here. I think, not more than a day's flight. He's causing quite a bit of concern with the humans in the area as he's terrorizing the people and stealing."

"Stealing? Is that all!" Then realizing that eagles don't steal and he was supposed to be reformed, Raven quickly added. "That's pretty shabby."

Bilgat chuckled. "When your thoughts are that loud I can't help but read them you know. Sounds to me like a crow calling a raven black. I seem to recall . . ."

"Yeah, yeah, yeah. What's past is past. What I really meant was, if he has true powers then he could be doing much worse than stealing. He could be changing things."

"Maybe he hasn't realized he can yet. After all it took you a while."

"Well then, the sooner we get there and put a stop to his tricks, the better. It certainly sounds like my brother, I wonder where he's been all these years."

"Farcry mentioned escape, as if he was trapped somewhere."

"That would explain it, I guess, but if he has the powers to change his situation then I'm surprised he didn't escape long before now."

"Ahhh, and how many times did you try to change things before you helped the frog, and how many worked?"

"Point taken."

"I reckon when the spirits returned to you, it might also have affected your brother in some way, and he managed to escape."

"You think there's a connection?"

"Well if he is your brother, then it's certainly a possibility."

"I really don't like the sound of that idea. He was mean you know. And I don't mean just chick rivalry, he was cruel. I hated him. Every time I think about those early days my head hurts. He used to pull out my pinfeathers as fast as they grew. I was nearly a year old before the feathers finally returned to the top of my head. I thought I was going to be bald forever."

Bilgat felt a huge surge of anger flow from the raven.

"Mean, cruel and vindictive, we were barely out of the nest, still fledglings really, when he took off for an early morning flight after being secretive about something for days. When he didn't return that night, mother and father searched, but he was never found. I figured he had finally picked on someone bigger than him and lost. Life improved tremendously after he was gone, I can tell you. By the way, where, exactly, are we going?"

They were flying over the last in the group of islands and, as the Pacific Ocean grew nearer, the sound of breaking waves became louder. The inlet widened. On the south side, a steep rugged cliff with a light on top was an indication to Bilgat that they should turn north, where the shoreline turned into a fine sandy beach that stretched out, and under, incoming surf. The short stubby trees bordering the beach were bent and twisted as though cowering away from the open expanse of sky. Driftwood piled up at the tide-line like a giant dam built by a monster-sized beaver. Sun-bleached timbers and enormous tangled root masses, jumbled together formed a sea wall, protecting the scrubby growth that was struggling to survive on the sand dunes behind.

Choosing a particularly large, twisted, white sculpture, Bilgat slowed his wing beats and, using his tail as an air brake, stretched out his talons, landing gracefully on the topmost root.

Raven circled to come in on a lower perch.

"You always get the best spot," he grumbled under his breath and probably would have complained louder but the view at ground level turned his irritation to awe.

"Just look at those waves," he gasped. Shouting to

make himself heard above the thunderous crashing of the water. "They're huge and there's hardly any wind, just a breeze really. What do you think makes them so big?"

Like Raven, Bilgat had never left the protection of the inside waters between the big island and the mainland. He had seen big waves before, but they were always accompanied by violent storms and high winds. These waves seemed gentle in comparison, even though they were enormous. For a start the water was clear blue instead of murky gray and, as each one smashed down on the fine white sand, it dissolved into a gentle ripple of foam that rolled up the beach, only to fall back and be absorbed by the next massive tower of water.

He was mesmerized. His respect for the ocean grew with each resounding crash. He could feel the power of the waves vibrate in his claws.

"Like I said before we landed, where to next?" Shouted the raven, unable to keep his eyes off the pounding surf, "and please don't tell me we have to fly over that."

"North," muttered Bilgat. He closed his eyes and opened them again as if he expected the scene to change.

Twisting his head and looking back at the scrubby, twisted pines he added, "And I don't think we should hang around too long. Looking at those trees, I wouldn't want to be here when the wind returns. Driftwood usually indicates the high tide line and we're sitting on it, so I would say the tide is going out right now. My guess is, that could all change when it turns and starts to come back in. The wind might come with it."

He lifted his head to search the sky and, as an afterthought, added, "I have to say though, the weather this morning is fantastic. Hard to believe; the sun is so warm it feels like summer"

"You're right, as usual, so lead on, but, summer weather or not, I'd rather fly along the shoreline here. Those waves look as though they could reach up and snatch you out of the sky. I've never trusted the ocean and I'm not about to start now, not after watching those waves."

"Well the directions didn't say we had to fly over the ocean, just head north till we get to a light on top of a cliff of black rock, so I don't see why not. It might take a bit longer if we fly around the bays instead of across them, but I agree, those waves bother me too. Besides there is probably a better updraft off these dunes than out over the sea."

That said, Bilgat took flight and, within minutes was joined by Raven. Together, the two birds turned north.

13
In Hot Water

A short flight
north, White Raven
woke early. Not because of the
rumble from an empty stomach, which had
been well filled the previous day, but to the rumble of
diesel engines. A few of the fishing boats were taking
advantage of the unusual break in the weather and were
heading out at dawn. The sound of reverse gears on the
large trawlers reverberated across the water, resembling
stones rattling down a drainpipe. A rather annoying
noise, which fortunately, didn't last long. Just long
enough to wake up a sleeping bird.

White Raven squinted at the sky. No fog, no rain, good. At least the sun was still behaving itself, although it did look a little worse for wear. With the clear sky, there was frost on the ground, but the wind was calm raising barely a ripple on the water. The gulls were darting around the trawlers. Daft idiots, he thought, the boats haven't caught any fish yet. You would think the fleet was coming in instead of going out.

He stretched his wings, tendons still a little tender from all the recent use. He was getting twinges in muscles he never knew he had. From his vantage point in the old, twisted arbutus tree he watched the activity on the docks as the fishermen cast off lines, leaving the seclusion of the little harbour, heading for the open sea.

Well there goes breakfast, he thought. The men who had offered him those delicious round balls had left with the boats, and with them, any hope of a free fish. As silence returned to the inlet, White Raven fluffed his feathers then dozed back to sleep, enjoying the luxury of a dry perch and at least a touch of warmth from the weak sun on his back.

He was woken a second time by the sound of crunching. There, directly below his tree, was an otter, munching on a large crab. He had already removed the vicious pinchers, which he had laid out on the rock beside him, and was now methodically cracking each of the legs in preparation for his breakfast feast.

White Raven watched and waited, finally, as the otter flipped over the carcass and tore into the body, he struck. Silently swooping from his branch, striking the otter square in the middle of it's back. His claws sunk into thick hide and his strong beak pecked hard at the otter's head before he soared back up to his branch of the tree. The otter squealed in pain and rolled onto it's back, looking to see what had attacked him. Not seeing White Raven, who crouched down quietly on his perch, he flipped back over, searching the water. The bird struck again. This time tearing away a chunk of fur and lacerating the otter's back. Screaming in pain, the otter swung around, clawing at his attacker, who flew above him, just out of reach. White Raven cackled in glee as the angry otter chased him across the clearing, his meal forgotten. Landing lightly on a low branch White Raven waited, the otter was almost within reach when he launched himself back across the rocks. The otter was fast, but not fast enough to stop the white bird snatching the cracked, juicy body of the crab in his beak and rising into the sky, well out of the reach of the furious animal.

The greedy bird flew up the steep slope until he was high above the inlet, landing on a rock bluff, as far away from the otter as possible. Years had passed since he had enjoyed such a large fresh crab and he tore into the exposed flesh. Tastier than the little sand crabs it was delicious.

There had been large crabs back on the beaches of that remote island when he first arrived, but within a month they were all gone, those he hadn't eaten, vanished. The months passed and their taste became a distant memory as the only crab from then on were dead, empty shells washed up on the beach. Life was finally good.

The sun continued to rise and, by the time White Raven flicked out the last piece of meat from one of the body crevasses, it was high overhead. The raven's beady eyes searched the remains of the crab shell, turning the empty carapace with his beak. There was nothing left, he had eaten it all. Finally, satisfied, he preened himself, finding a few pieces that had stuck to his feathers.

Twisting his neck in an attempt to reach the last of

the crab meat, he felt his muscles complain again. The frost on the rock under his feet probably didn't help. He scowled at the sky. Even though the sun was there, he felt it really wasn't putting much effort into warming the earth. The fact that it was still early spring, and the sun's rays had much further to travel to reach this small cove on the northern part of the world, was not something that was of interest to the bird. His main concern was his own comfort.

He gave a big sigh, Oh well, he thought, it's better than rain at least, although I could do with a bath.

With a hop and a flap he took to the air. He could remembered seeing a small creek at the end of the bay, which wasn't far, and decided to go and check it out. He needed to get any remaining crab pieces off his feathers before they got too dry and stuck for good.

The morning air was crisp and invigorating but to aching muscles it was just another grievance. It wasn't long before he spotted the creek and did a circle, landing beside a small pool created by the water before it tumbled over the rim of rocks and fell into the sea. To the white raven's disgust, there was ice all around the edge of the bank. Just looking at it made his bones ache in protest. How was anyone supposed to get clean when the water was so damn cold? The irritation triggered a small thought.

White Raven looked harder at the pool and thought again. The thought swelled, rather proud of itself. It was a good thought, worthy of some serious consideration. Well it had worked before. Why not try it again?

Focusing on his own reflection on the surface of the pool, and putting all his aches, pains, frustrations and anger into it, White Raven concentrated his demands on the water. He closed his eyes forcing his anger deeper and deeper. Deep in the very core of the earth his voice was heard.

The element was a solitary being. When the world was young, he had danced upon its surface with wild fury. Night and day, he had roared and raced around in free abandon. But, as the years passed and the centuries faded he grew tired and his enthusiasm cooled, then hardened. Moisture formed on the earth's crust and a second element, Water, was born.

A few more centuries came and went and the water became an ocean. The two elements were at war with each other. One being old and weak, the other young, fresh and full of life. The first element was Fire and it receded, sliding underground to make a home at the very core of the planet. There he had control and, although confined to a much smaller space, he was able to regain his strength and fight back. It was an upvent battle. He spewed lava onto the ocean floor, forming sea mounds and sometimes managed to get to the surface, creating ferocious fountains of fire and ash, his hot breath creeping across the newly formed land. But eventually he met with the second element, Water, and his lava cooled.

Sometimes Water would find a small crack in his armour and creep into his lair, but in such a confined space the invader was soon discovered and sent packing, back to the surface in the form of a steaming hot geyser.

Fire hated Water, his one and only enemy. Everything on the surface contained water. Water had created life and the many-celled creatures that now walked the planet. His planet.

He was stoking the coals of one of his newest volcanoes when Fire felt the call. Not surprisingly, it was a call from a many-celled creature. He had listened to calls like this in the past, demands to pour his

---

brimstone on another of the beings, or for his fire to destroy some perceived enemy. Pitiful demands really. What was in it for him? Nothing. They were calls he usually ignored.

He was about to return to stirring up his lava when he felt the pull again. Only this time it was much stronger. He paused and felt the anger. He could taste it; here was a kindred soul. He grew curious. He sensed this was no ordinary multi-celled creature. And the anger was focused on his old enemy, Water. He missed the freedom he had on the surface, maybe this was his ticket back. Here too was another being that hated Water. Well why not? He wasn't really busy and, who knew, it might lead to a lasting relationship.

The first thing White Raven felt was a small shudder that rippled through the rock he was standing on. Then he smelt sulphur. His eyes flew open.

The pool itself didn't look any different except the ice around the edges had vanished. He looked closer and spotted a small wisp of steam rising from the centre. He dipped one chilled claw in. He yanked it back. The water wasn't just warm it was HOT. Almost too hot.

Tentatively he tried again. It took him some time to adjust to the temperature as he eased in, slowly immersing himself.

"Ahhhhhh . . . hhhhhh," he let out a deep sigh of pure bliss. Never, even on a hot summer day, had the white raven felt so warm. His aches and pains vanished and his mind floated off into warm, pleasant oblivion.

White Raven's obvious pleasure was not lost on the element. Until now, he had never been in such close contact with a many-celled creature and hadn't realized they were so emotional. He could feel the bottled-up fire within the being. It was pumping a red river throughout its body, and red was his favourite colour.

Yessss . . . finally he had found a kindred being and he reveled in the unspoken praise. It made him feel like a god and he didn't want it to end. He sensed this creature understood banishment and the desire for freedom: he reached out to his new-found friend.

White Raven felt his heart hammer in his chest as the temperature in the pool rose. His skin tingled and a strange sensation crept up through his body. His sense of self-preservation took over, even as his mind was lost somewhere in a state of bliss. He scrambled out of the pool as the temperature continued to rise. Steam rose where the creek fed into the pool and bubbles gurgled up from the centre. The smell of sulphur thickened. The pool was no longer hot; it was beginning to boil.

The cool air helped the raven pull his mind back into his head. He stared back at the pool. Had he really done that? A torrent of unanswerable questions flooded his brain as he stepped to the edge of the rock and watched the steaming water tumble over the rocks and into the ocean.

Already there were several crabs and assorted sea life floating up to the surface, some struggling to resubmerge. They eventually gave up and died, drifting out to join the seaweed and other debris at the tide line.

A very confused White Raven watched, fascinated as fountains of hot steam shot up into the trees. He idly threw a couple of escaping crabs back into the boiling water. The air escaping from their shells sounded like a scream as each crab cooked and turned bright red.

Had he done this? Almost stewed himself, but if he had, he had power. The feathers around his beak curled in a twisted smile.

14
A Whale of a Journey

The flight north was proving interesting for Bilgat and Raven. The shoreline was dramatically different to their homelands. Every now and then great, craggy, rock pinnacles towered out of the sea. Most were barren, but some had scraggy trees on top, their roots clinging to every crack and fissure in their struggle to survive. The waves had carved tunnels into the base of the rocks forming great caves and arches that were crowded with seabirds, many types neither Raven or Bilgat had seen before.

The most interesting was a chubby, black, duck-size, bird with a white chest and a colourful beak. His short, stubby wings flapped so hard when he took flight it was almost funny. By mid-afternoon they arrived at a wide bay that was the mouth of a large inlet, and decided to stop for a rest.

"The waves are not so large here," commented Bilgat, "just swells. I think we could cut across. I haven't seen any sign of black cliffs yet and the shoreline here is mostly covered in sand dunes. If we fly across, it will be much shorter. If we don't find the light soon, we may have to stop for the night. I guess we could ask one of the locals how much further it is."

"I hope you weren't thinking of asking any of the gulls. This lot seems worse than the flocks at home, if that's at all possible. All they seem to be doing is flying in circles till we get near, then they all take off like a bunch of frightened house sparrows."

"No, I was thinking more along the lines of asking those small black birds with the rainbow coloured beaks. They look intelligent, and they know how to fish. Have you noticed the way they use their wings for flippers when they dive? They actually chase the fish instead of waiting till one gets close to the surface. I bet a few other birds wish they could do that. I've seen a few of the divers swim underwater, but these guys are the best I've ever seen and that bill of theirs can store a lot of fish.

"Hmmm." Raven didn't seem to be listening and Bilgat gave him a quizzical look.

"What's up?" He asked, trying to be polite and not probe the raven's thoughts."

"I'm not sure," replied Raven. "I thought I heard a strange cry coming from that smooth rock out there in the middle of the bay."

Bilgat looked across the water and laughed. "That's not a rock," he chuckled. "It's a whale. Look, it's moving."

As if it had heard them and knew it was being watched, the rock spouted a jet of water.

"So it is."

As the rock inched forward through the water, Raven noticed a small dorsal fin protruding from the top of the gray lump.

"But what kind of whale is that? It's huge. It doesn't look like one of our blackfish. For the size of the body, that dorsal fin is tiny."

Bilgat didn't answer. When Raven tore his attention from the whale, he saw the blank look in Bilgat's eyes and knew he was doing one of his mind-reading tricks. When his friend's eyes screwed up with pain he grew concerned and gave him a prod with his beak.

"Heh, wake up. BILGAT, WAKE UP," he shouted.

Bilgat shuddered and stumbled on his perch. He flapped his wings to regain his balance and did a strange side-step along the branch and back.

"Wow," He shook his head, stretched his neck and took a huge gulp of air. "Remind me not to try and mind read a whale again. I feel as if I drowned."

"Serve you right if you did. I had to peck you to get you out of it. If I hadn't been around you would have been sunk, literally."

"Thanks, I think."

"Well, after all that trouble, did you find out anything?"

"Actually yes. For a start he's just a youngster, not more that a fledgling really, he's confused and in pain. One minute he wants his mother the next he wants to beach himself. Beyond that I can't make much sense of his baby talk. There's no question, he's definitely lost."

"Well, if he wants his pod he should be going the other way. I don't see any other whales in the bay."

Bilgat's eyes searched the horizon, "THERE." He shouted so loud Raven screeched in surprise.

Standing on one foot, he put his head down and, using his claw, scratched at the feathers around the ear that was closest to Bilgat.

"I'm not deaf you know," he complained, "or at least I wasn't till now."

"I'm sorry. I guess I'm still under the influence of my visit with youngster out there and got a bit excited. Look, out on the horizon. There is a large pod of whales."

Raven looked out to sea just as something very large rose out of the water only to fall back with a huge splash.

"They're whales alright. I could never figure out why they do that. You would think they were trying to fly. So now what? He's down there heading for some beach whilst Ma and Pa swim off into the sunset. Got any ideas?"

"I guess you becoming a whale is out of the question."

"After seeing what you experienced, absolutely not. On the other claw, maybe I could go out and have a little chat with him. If you stay aloft and keep an eye on the pod, maybe I can steer him back out to sea."

"A little chat? About what for beaks sake?"

"Well most kids think a lot about food, so how about 'what he had for lunch'. That should be a good starter."

"Food!! Don't tell me you're hungry again. Besides I can tell you he didn't have any lunch or breakfast for that matter. In fact, it seems he hasn't eaten in days. From what I managed to get from his thoughts, he doesn't eat fish, just a type of shrimp, only very small and something called plankton."

"Well no wonder he hasn't eaten for days, who could get fat on that?"

'They do, that's what these whales eat."

"You're joking? No, I can see your not. Oh well, that's all I really needed to know anyway, so I'll go out for a nice visit and you head up into the wide blue yonder and lead the way."

Before Bilgat could question him any more, Raven unfolded his wings and took off, soaring up into the sky, heading out over the water toward the wallowing whale. As he neared, he slowed his wing beats and descended gently to land on the back of the baby giant.

Startled, and more than a little afraid, the whale began to dive when, with surprising clarity, he sensed a huge mass of krill surface in the water behind him. His hunger proved stronger than his concern over the strange weight on his back and he turned in a huge circle and began to head back toward the open sea and the tantalizing scent of a good meal.

"That's more like it. Glad to see I've got your attention, I was beginning to think you were dead."

Hearing a strange voice from above surprised the whale, but whales don't do anything at great speed, including thinking. The young whale exhaled slowly and the weight on his back shifted suddenly.

"Hey, warn me next time won't you. I'm soaked. Now I've got you turned around, we can get you back to your family."

"Hungry."

"Yes, I know, I heard."

"Pain."

Raven peered down at the slow moving island. Even for a whale it was moving at an incredibly slow pace.

"What kind of pain," he inquired.

"Tangled, hurt, roll, you see."

With that the whale started to roll onto its back. Raven barely had time to leap into the air before his perch was submerged beneath the waves. As the underside of the whale came into view he saw a large mass of nylon line tangled from one flipper to the other. The huge loops that crisscrossed his belly must have been there so long, some of the line had cut into the flesh of the young whale.

Ouch, thought Raven. Well at least the line is an easy fix, the rest will have to heal itself.

Raven concentrated. Within seconds, the line that was wrapped around the young whale dissolved into a tangled mass of eel grass that broke away with each passing wave.

I'm getting better at this, he thought cheerfully, and, as the whale righted itself, he asked, "feel any better?"

"Free? Gone! Hungry."

The whale's speed increased as he realized his movements were no longer causing him pain. He renewed his efforts toward the food with enthusiasm. The pain was forgotten which seemed to be the one thing that whales can do with any speed.

Further out to sea, the pod of whales slowed. As though sensing their youngster was returning, the leading whale breached and turned, causing the rest of the pod to slow and swim in a huge lazy circle, waiting. The second he heard his family calling, the smell of food vanished from the water and the young whale realized he was no longer alone.

Flying to the head of the pod, Raven circled above the largest of the whales.

"Your youngster is heading back. I've gotten rid of the tangled mass of fishing line that was cutting into him but, I'm afraid he is very hungry," he called down.

The massive mammal rolled on its side and one small eye peered up at the raven.

"A raven, helped my grandson?"

There was puzzlement in the deep, echoing voice. As a slow wave of understanding flooded his brain, old memories surfaced.

"I do believe the spirits are with us again." It was more of a statement than a question.

"Has a transformer returned? If so, I thank you." The old whale seemed in the habit of answering his own questions.

"You're welcome," said Raven, "but like I said he's very hungry."

"We will rest for a while. There is a protected bay not far from here with lots of feed. He won't be hungry for long. There we will wait till he is healed and strong enough to continue on our migration. I am curious though, why did you help him? It's totally out of character."

"Maybe I thought he was dead. There would have been enough meat on him to keep me fed for weeks," snapped Raven.

The old whale's eye twinkled. "I don't think so lad, that's an old one. You can't fool me, I've been around too long and seen many a raven in my time. You're not like the rest. For a start you seem much smarter. The last raven who tried that trick almost drowned."

* * *

An old story tells of a Raven who was hungry, so hungry that when he spotted a humpback whale on the surface of the ocean with a spear in it's side, the thought of an easy meal spurred him into a scheme to capture the huge creature. Thinking the whale was almost dead, the raven transformed himself into a giant Thunderbird and flew down, sinking his talons into the back of the whale,

*intending on dragging him to the beach. Unfortunately
for the raven, the whale was only sleeping and the shock
of claws piercing his already tender hide caused him
to sound. He dove deep, and the raven, with claws still
embedded in the back of the whale, was dragged down
beneath the waves and almost died.*

*The moral of this story is not to be greedy and bite off
more than you can chew.*

* * *

The old whale's eye was almost closed, the lid
reduced it to a slit, as he caught sight of Bilgat who had
flown lower to join the party.

"Well, well! Just like old times." Rumbled the whale.

"Good afternoon sir," said Bilgat

"Good afternoon to you Great Eagle. Who would
believe it, the two of you back together again flying side

by side."

"Not quite sir, Great Eagle is my great, great grandfather and Raven here is the great, great grandson of Raven."

"That explains it. The pair of you do seem rather young, even for a transformer. Well, thanks to you, my grandson is back with his mother and we all owe you a huge debt."

"Then sir, maybe you can tell us how much further we have to fly to reach the high black cliffs with a light on top."

"Certainly. You're almost there. It's just around the next headland. There's a large bay protected from the incoming waves by a long thin island. That's the bay we will be staying in. Beyond that are the cliffs. I suspect we will be in the bay for several days. We've all been worried and upset about junior. When he vanished last night we were afraid he had chosen 'the great beach'."

"The great beach?" Raven interrupted.

"It's where whales go when they decide to end the pain."

"Oh," Raven remembered how close the young whale was swimming to the sandy shoreline.

"I'm glad we spotted him before he reached the shore then." He admitted. "I'm not sure how I would have gotten him off a beach."

"It certainly would have been much harder, but," and the eye twinkled as it peered up into the eyes of the hovering Raven, "you would have figured something out."

The picture of a giant bird lifting a whale in his claws, drifted into Raven's head. It seemed so real that, for a moment, Raven was mesmerized at the vision.

Seeing Raven staring at the horizon, the whale decided it was time to move on.

"Now it seems everyone is back into formation." The whale blew a short fountain of water into the air, being careful not to spray too close to the two birds. "So the sooner we get to the feeding grounds the happier this youngster will be. Wherever you're going, I wish you a safe journey and, remember, if I can ever be of any assistance to you in your travels, don't hesitate to ask."

With that the whale rolled back, blew another fountain of water into the air then surged forward, leading his family toward food and shelter.

Bilgat and Raven rose into the sky together, neither one talking to the other as, in unison, they flew across the water toward the protruding headland.

The gap in the black cliff face was narrow, although not as narrow as the cut through the mountains, and the two birds entered the sheltered waters together, flying wing tip to wing tip. The day was fading as night closed in but there was enough light for the two birds to spot an indent in the steep rock wall, just inside the entrance. There, a tiny, almost apologetic beach clung to the craggy shoreline. A large Douglas-fir had found a strong footing beside a small creek that tumbled and fell down the cliff face before vanishing into the pebbles and sand. They needed no words or thought transfers; both birds turned as one, flying up into the branches of the tall tree. Food would have to wait until morning.

Raven settled onto a branch and drifted into a deep sleep. The evening was calm and the air was humid, hardly the kind of evening you would expect in early spring when, even on the warmest days, the evening chill usually brought on a night frost. Bilgat sat for a while watching his friend, thinking.

What was all that about a bird carrying a whale? He had seen the picture clearly in Raven's head. It brought back memories of his chickhood when Grandfather told them the stories of the past, stories about great birds of thunder and huge creatures of the deep. Mythical creatures that hadn't survived to the present day, creatures that had vanished along with the spirits.

His eyes closed and the gray band of sleep crept up from deep within his feathers. The last thought that niggled at his conscious was, but the spirits are back.

15
Eggs for the taking

Whilst Bilgat and Raven were saving a whale, a little further north the small town bustled with traffic and people. Bells were ringing, a group of children played on the beach, and there was a hub of activity in the town square.

Time to check things out, thought White Raven. His stomach was full, his feathers were healed, and he felt good. The morning had been entertaining, he hadn't had so much fun in a long time. It was almost mid-day and the movements across the bay peaked his interest. The sleepy little hamlet was full of action and, from the experience of the last few days, the interesting things these people did was an endless source of entertainment.

To the humans, it was a special day. A day to celebrate, a day that had no significance to animals at all because animals are not religious the way people are. True, some animals believed in the spirits, the spirits are everywhere, but animals don't celebrate spiritual days the same way people do. The meaning of Christmas would confuse them and the significance of today being Easter meant nothing to White Raven as he flew with leisurely swoops across the water.

A group of ladies gathered together laughing, each wore a ridiculous hat. There was a human dressed in a giant size rabbit costume carrying balloons. Across the park, in a children's play area, another group of ladies were scattering sparkly objects into the tall grasses and hiding them in the bushes.

Curious, White Raven settled in a nearby tree and watched. When the ladies finished, he flew in for a closer look. As they left the play area laughing and chatting to each other, none of the ladies looked back. If they had, they would have seen a strange sight. A large, white raven rolling a shiny coloured Easter egg out from under a bush.

White Raven didn't know what to make of it. All around him, scattered everywhere, were sparklies. White Raven LOVED sparklies. They were round and hard and shaped like eggs. Next to sparklies, he really liked eggs. He could still remember the taste of the fresh gull eggs he used to steal way back-when, before that fateful flight north. Egg sparklies, and there were so many. The most beautiful sparkly eggs he had ever seen, and the ladies had hidden them all away.

Whatever kind of bird laid eggs that sparkled? Why hide them in the bushes? Were they dangerous? They didn't look dangerous. The women had hidden them, but they were easy to find. He could have done a better job of hiding them; much better

He shook his head, too much thinking and not enough doing. He'd show them. He was really good at hiding things. He snatched up the nearest egg, now they were all his, and as fast as he could, he gathered them into piles then flew with as many as he could carry in his beak to the nearest rooftop.

He lost track of how many trips he made. His muscles ached but the excitement of the hunt masked the pain. As he searched out any remaining eggs he noticed children gathering outside the gate. There was a high hedge around the play area that blocked all view of the white raven. No-one had seen him . . . yet.

He scooped up the last of the eggs from the grass and, spotting one more on the seat of the swing, was about to fly over to it when the gate burst open and twenty or so excited children crowded into the play area. He almost dropped the eggs he carried as he jumped into the air, narrowly missing the monkey bars and catching his wing tip as he flew between dangling ropes.

One of the larger children spotted him and pointed a grubby little finger at him just as he cleared the top of the hedge. Too late, they saw the eggs he carried. As puzzled youngsters ran aimlessly around the playground, one toddler picked up the egg from the seat of the swing. He held it high in the air calling to his mother in joy. A call that turned to one of pain as the white raven swooped in and stole the last egg from his chubby little hand. Cawing with glee, White Raven circled the playground, diving at the frightened children

who ran in panic back to their astonished mothers.
A few of the ladies ran into the play area waving their
arms, whilst others consoled the toddlers. Quickly bored
with the new game, White Raven flew back up to the
rooftop to enjoy his windfall.

His pile was magnificent. It glistened in the noonday
sun. White Raven settled down beside his treasure
enjoying the warmth that radiated off the tar and gravel
rooftop. Spreading out his wings he mantled his eggs.
Every pinion could feel the heat and the raven rested his
head on the top of his hoard.

The sun looked down on the scene. He was tired,
and he wanted a rest. In his befuddled brain he knew it
was the fault of this bird, this unusual white raven. It
was as if the bird had frightened away all the clouds and
had some sort of control over the morning mist, forcing
him to keep shinning. Without the mist, he had to get
up early. Without clouds to hide behind, he couldn't
rest, no afternoon nap, no siesta. Resentment boiled,
fueling the heat of his solar flares. His anger radiated
as hot as mid summer. He glared down on the rooftop.
With warmth coming from above and below, a very smug
White Raven snoozed whilst around him his eggs slowly
melted.

Afternoon wore on and Sun dropped in the sky, if anyone with the right kind of glasses could look closer they would see a rather smug look on his yellow face. The mountains were getting closer and soon he would have a chance to rest and put up his flares.

It wasn't just the strange smell that finally awoke White Raven, it was a painful kink in his neck. The warmth had penetrated White Raven's feathers, lulling him into a stupor. The unusual smell wasn't bad, just different. He couldn't place it. He inhaled deeply. Whatever it was, it was close, intoxicating, and quite pleasant really. It was a sensual type of aroma, one that had flavour. It was a happy smell and, as he dozed, he was wrapped in a feeling of soft, oozing comfort. His rather hard lumpy pillow had transformed to cradle his head. It was a pleasurable rich . . . sticky feeling?

He struggled to open his eyes. The smell had grown so strong he could taste it in every breath. It befuddled his brain. Shaking his head was out of the question, the smallest movement caused the pain in his kinked neck to shoot all the way down to his tail feathers. Moving his eyes as slowly as possible, he looked around. His beak was so close to the ground that gravel was at eye level. The thief realized his mound of eggs had vanished.

Someone had crept in during his sleep and stolen his treasure. Anger overrode the pain in his neck and he lifted his head, searching the rooftop for the thief. His feathers felt heavy and, as his mind became clear, the last of the sleep swept from it's corners, he registered the fact that, besides the pain in his neck, he really didn't feel quite right. He struggled to identify the problem and came up with just one word . . . sticky.

White Raven tried to lift a wing. It was a painful move that caused him to screech in pain as several

---

of the older feathers in his neck were torn from their shafts. He stared at a glutinous, brown mess that surrounded him. It dripped from his feathers, crept between his claws like thick oozing mud and, mixed in the middle of it all, floated colourful bits of sparklies.

The taste of the brown was on his beak and made him feel weak and dizzy. He struggled to lift himself out of the pool of brown. His sparkly eggs had all broken. They hadn't been stolen they had . . . melted? Melted and stuck to his feathers. Bits of silver sparkly stuck to his chest and neck along with gravel from the rooftop. The brown had coated him all the way down to his tail pinions. He tried to preen himself but the taste and smell was overwhelming. He felt his heart race and his befuddled senses told him the brown was poison.

Whilst the White Raven struggled, a happy sun sank behind the trees. He giggled to himself. The extra work and effort had paid off. He could hardly wait till morning to see how that nasty bird got out of that one. It would have been worth it to work overtime to stay and watch but, to his very core, tiredness prevailed and told him it was time to rest. He had to agree. Searching the open sky for his brother, the moon, he was sorry there was no sign of him. Pity. Although they only spoke on rare occasions, he knew his brother would have also enjoyed the joke.

The air cooled, the shadows lengthened, and White Raven struggled as the brown stiffened. He tried to raise a wing but the weight of the goop sapped his strength. The cooler he became the harder the brown was to move.

A group of seagulls, probably the same ones as the day before, gathered along the edge of the rooftop. For gulls they were incredibly silent. Well! What could you say to a big white bird with a cruel looking pink beak and angry red eyes, that glared at you through feathers covered in goo, embedded with pretty sparklies?

They were stunned! They were screechless!

Warmth melts the stuff. The thought finally penetrated through to what little sense White Raven had left in his intoxicated brain. His eyes searched the top of the building. The light was fading and his neck feathers so stiff he had to turn his whole body to see it all. With a great sigh of relief he spotted the hot air shaft. It seemed a lot further away than he remembered, but there it was, halfway across the rooftop. Now that his eyes had located it, he could hear the soft rumble of the fan.

The journey across that small stretch of tar and gravel was as bad as that struggle up the beach. Maybe worse. This time he had an audience; more herring gulls gathered on the rooftop. Bits of sparkly and brown chipped, dripped, and splattered as White Raven hopped toward the shaft.

"He looks like one of those trees, people decorate mid winter." snickered one of the gulls.

"Oh but he's really pretty, don't you think?" Cackled another. "Pretty stupid."

"I like the glittery red bit stuck on top of his head. It reminds me of the lights that stop the traffic."

"He'd stop the traffic alright." Croaked the largest of the gulls.

Flopping down in front of the vent, White Raven's collapsed form looked like an old sack of dirty laundry. To the watchers, he looked dead. The brown softened as White Raven rested and gathered his strength. Unfortunately, while it softened, the fumes intensified.

The gulls had lost all fear and their whispers grew louder. Their cackles of laughter, as he had struggled across the roof top, were not lost on the raven. His eyes were streaming when he finally felt recuperated enough to give himself a good shake. He had seen wolves do it; it worked for them.

A few of the more curious gulls, who had crept up behind him, were hit with a spray of brown before they had a chance to move. The group rose into the air, screaming as brown goop and sparklies flew in all directions.

Anger gave him strength and he lunged at the closest, and last, gull struggling to leave. The brown had hit the gull in the face, temporarily blinding him. The stunned creature didn't stand a chance as White Raven attacked.

The screaming of the gulls intensified as they looked down on their fallen comrade. Whether the white raven had broken their brother's neck, or just stunned him with that angry blow from his beak, was hard to determine from forty feet in the air. In shock they circled.

White Raven felt tricked. He could see it now. Someone had deliberately left those poisoned eggs for him to find. Something was trying to kill him. Maybe spirits were watching him and waiting. Yes, that was it; waiting for the brown to creep through his feather shafts. He flapped his wings harder and, although some of the smaller feathers were still stuck together, he could feel that most of the weight had gone and he had lift. With a supreme effort he leapt into the air. The gulls fled.

The sun had gone to bed and the moon was just peeking around the top of the mountain. It had a grin on its face but White Raven was too exhausted to do anything more than add one more name to the revenge list. Oh yes, he would have his revenge for this.

He knew he would need to draw on every last muscle in his body to get across the water to his tree on the other side of the bay.

His flight was staggered, jerky and off balance. His vision was impaired and he could feel his heart still racing. As if sensing his weakness, an evening mist crept up from the waterline as the last of the daylight faded. White Raven didn't care; he just wanted his nice cozy branch and a good night's sleep. The brown so confused his brain that he completely forgot how his wishful thinking had changed things on the beach, how his anger had cleared away the wind and given him strength to fly. Resentment so filled his brain with thoughts of revenge that he completely forgot how he had forced the sun to shine and cause an icy pool to boil. If he had remembered, this story would probably have a far different ending. But then, maybe he really didn't know how he had done any of those things, or maybe he just didn't believe.

The rising mist blanketed the wharf. White Raven hit an old piling with such a resounding thud any other bird would have died instantly with a broken neck. It was several minutes before his senses returned and he found himself lying on his back at the end of a decrepit, disintegrating piece of old dock.

Behind him was the remains of an old, neglected boat shed. Many of the side planks were missing, but some sheets of corrugated iron still clung to the roof. The rafters at the rear of the shed looked dry. It would be a good place to rest and recuperate.

It was a struggle to get his wings to work again in synchronization. He flapped. He staggered. He hopped and finally managed to get his body off the debris covered planking and into the air but his landing on the cross beam of the shed was probably the worst in bird history. With his brain fighting reality and brown bunnies hopping out of the mist, he hit the centre of the old roof. How he managed to miss the cross members as he flew in, we'll never know but he didn't miss them as he fell. He hit and rolled off two of the struts before he landed on the central beam, by sheer luck, the right way up. His claws instinctively gripped the perch, clinging, clasping. They stopped his fall. All movement ceased. Even the rising dust froze as White Raven's claws gripped and penetrated the old wood.

Hidden deep within the old boathouse, the white raven was a very sorry, and somewhat frightening, sight. Odd remnants of the brown caused feathers to stick out at strange angles. His eyes, barely visible through slits, were the colour of blood and he breathed in ragged gasps. As he slumped on the beam and fell into a stupor you might wonder if he was breathing his last.

Will he make it do you think?
Unfortunately, yes, his heart is strong
Pity
Yes

Another set of eyes, a bit closer to the ground, had also watched as White Raven flew at full, if a somewhat erratic speed, into the piling. They waited, hardly daring to blink, wondering if the raven had indeed snapped his neck. They followed his staggered flight into the building and, when the flapping and banging inside the boat shed finally ceased, they waited. From a tall cedar towering above the marina nothing more could be seen, or heard.

As quiet as an owl, the old eagle flew down and landed on the roof of the shed. He peered through one of the rusty holes. He might be slow on the wing but his eyesight was still superb and a very curious moon was helping with soft rays of light that penetrated shadows.

The huddled lump of feathers below him was still breathing.

Pity.

16
The Meeting

Fog crept through the harbour entrance. It was early in the morning. For days he'd been forced to stay offshore rather than risk being dried by the sun. It was out of character for the fog, and unseasonable for the weather. Each day the sun had risen, dragged into the sky, as if being pulled by a string. Then yesterday afternoon something had happened and last night Fog heard a message being sent from Moon to say that Sun could probably have a sleep-in as the brown-white bird was down for the count.

What ever that meant!

Fog really didn't care, it was just nice to be back on land and feel the trees as they brushed through his tendrils. He hugged the cliff face and curled up on the small beach. High above, a foghorn sounded. It was music, a song that was sung every time he came ashore the world over. To him it was a song of welcome.

Above, three birds roosted in a tall fir tree. Two were fast asleep, the other, an old eagle he had seen many times over the years, watched him. Although his memory was foggy, he vaguely remembered when the old eagle's wife had flown out over the sea; never to return.

Most of Fog's memories were vague, shrouded in a white mist, but his recollection of that day was clearer than most. A sky, blue and cloudless; the Sun warning the beach whilst he gathered steam rising from the wet rocks. An eagle flying over, so low to the ground, her wing beats had sent him flying. Being flattened into the rocks caused him to spill his morning's work. He remembered waiting for her return, gathering moisture around him. A long wait, and by the end of the day, he had formed a heavy mist blanketing the coastline. What his intentions were, was no longer clear, but he never saw her again.

He sensed the old eagle's glaring, accusatory eyes. Suddenly he didn't feel quite so comfortable.

Thinking it was time to move on, Fog uncurled himself, stretched, then drifted across the bay toward the small boat harbour on the far side. He felt the eagle's probing pupils follow him as he slid across the docks and hid between the boats. Those eyes made him feel guilty, as if he was responsible for something.

He liked this little bay. The wind rarely bothered to come in, preferring to race up and down the wide open beaches. Maybe he should head inland for a bit, until that old bird moved on. With that thought, he rose up, drifted across the beach, up the bank, between the border of trees, eventually arriving at the village. There, he settled down again, shrouding the buildings in a white veil.

Eagles are very sensitive to the thoughts of others. The old eagle was careful to shield his thoughts while Bilgat slept but, when the fog settled at the foot of the cliff, he forgot himself. That same fog had hung around after his wife left. Those wisps on the beach had drifted together to became a dense, almost impenetrable mass after she left the shoreline. He sensed the anger and, when she didn't return, often wondered if the fog had somehow trapped her.

Bilgat woke to a loud and angry, "GO AWAY." bouncing through his skull. At the end of the limb was an old eagle glaring down through the branches. What he was glaring at, and why, was a bit of a mystery. All Bilgat could see was a morning mist on the beach. He stretched a wing and shook the sleep out of his eyes, surprised to see the foggy tendrils lift up and drift off across the bay.

The old bird relaxed and settled down on his perch, his eyes coming back to the visitors.

"Morning," said Bilgat. "Can I assume I am speaking to Eagle Farcry?"

"That's me, but you can drop the formality. I'm just glad to see you finally arrived, although I wish there were more of you."

"So I take it, it's not us you want to 'go away'?"

"No, no. It was that damned miserable fog; it makes me nervous. Ever since my wife . . . but there, you didn't come all this way to hear my problems. White Raven is recuperating across the bay in an old boat shed. He stole brown treat food that was shaped like eggs and wrapped in shiny coloured papers, from the kids yesterday. Now he's suffering from the brown sickness. Oh, and he might have killed a gull."

"The brown-poisonous-human-treat food?"

"The same. I guess wherever he's from, no-one told him about the sickness that birds and animals get from some of the people foods. Especially the treat foods."

"AAGH. Who's talking?" Raven blinked at the eagles huddled together on the end of the branch.

"Morning Raven. We have a visitor. Meet Farcry, Master Crier and the sender of the messages."

Raven scowled at the old eagle. He had a similar stance and cast of feather as Great Eagle. The beak was pale and cracked with age, but he had the same clear, piercing eyes that could drill holes in your head.

Raven was tired and more than a little hungry. He didn't feel like going through the niceties of etiquette. Not this early in the day and certainly not on an empty stomach.

"The sun's not even up yet." He complained, yawning as he twisted his neck from side to side in a halfhearted attempt to get the blood flowing to his brain. He was stiff, sore, and his feathers were refusing to separate as he stretched.

The old eagle tipped his own head to one side as if he was listening for something.

"Don't you start," Raven snapped, giving his head a shake. "I've had enough brain scanning, or washing, or whatever you call it, to last a life time. You want to know about me, ask your buddy here. I'm off to find some breakfast," and, before Farcry could say a word, he took flight.

Raven's instinct took him across the water, to the far side of the bay. He didn't much care where he went; he just needed to get away from the probing eyes and curious looks for a while. Part of his brain was still asleep as his eyes scanned the shoreline, his mind

---

The White Raven

assessing the chances of finding food.

Below him, a tide line spread across the water and, as he flew over, he noticed that, instead of the usual seaweed, it was full of dead shore crabs, bullheads, shrimp, and sand fleas. Curious, he flew lower following the line of debris. Not talented at scooping up things from the ocean, he looked for the source. Before long, he came to a beach that was steaming with hot water flowing over the rocks, cascading into the sea. Careful to stay out of the line of hot water, he landed on the shore. There was dead sea life scattered all over the rocks. With an easy breakfast on his mind, he pecked at the closest crab. Just as quickly, he spat it out. Yuck, it tasted like nothing he had ever eaten before. The water smelled strange to a raven who had never encountered sulphur. His eyes followed the stream of hot water up into the trees. A few hops and he found himself standing at the edge of a pool of bubbling water.

"A white raven did this." A large male raccoon emerged from the undergrowth. "My family den is underneath these bushes. Been here for generations." He scowled at the rising steam. "That was our fresh water supply. We'll have to move now. Can't drink that, besides it's dangerous for the little-uns. You want to be careful," he warned. "Don't stand too close. Every now and then it shoots a fountain of scalding hot water into the air."

"Did you actually see him do it?" Asked Raven, stepping back from the water's edge. Curious and more than a little disturbed that his brother had the power to make such a change, he frowned, as he questioned the raccoon.

"Well, not exactly, he didn't wave a stick or anything. He stood there muttering about the ice and cold when suddenly it started to steam. He actually got in it and was having a great bath when all of a sudden he shot out of the water as if his tail was on fire. Then the bubbles started and it was as if the water was angry. When it shot steam in the air, that white bird just stood to one side and watched the suffering. Damned bird was enjoying it; started throwing live crabs into the hot water. Crabs scream you know, when they cook. Had the wife take the youngsters away. Couldn't have them see that. Then when he got bored of the game he just left us without a care."

The raccoon shook in anger. "Look at the death that pool has caused already. If it continues it will only get worse. The water in the bay will warm and soon we won't have any fish. Then we'll all have to leave."

Raven studied the pool. His brother had done this. It was hard to imagine. Did he really have that much power?. Could he fix it?

The element could feel the strength that emanated from the raven standing on the bank. Something told him this bird was different. There was no raging anger in his soul. No hate. No resentment. There was, however, a powerful aura that surrounded the bird. A strength that comes from within; a strong sense of purpose.

As the raven moved close to the edge of the pool, the element shrank away. He waited. The bubbles that were actively rising to the surface of the pool slowed. He sensed the power; could feel a tension in the air. He didn't have to wait long. A chilling mind-numbing cold attacked his very core.

The element had never felt such cold. He shriveled back in horror and fear, sinking down through the crack in the rocks to the warmth of his subterranean home.

He should have known better. All the multi-celled

creatures were concerned with was their own comfort. The next time one called upon his abilities he would give them a real shock. Yes, he would let them know who had the power. Just wait. Next time.

I was wondering how long you were going to let that go on.
You said the high council tries to avoid too many deaths.
Me?
What gave you the idea I could do anything?
We have no control over the elements.
Did they not teach you anything?

Ice began to reform around the pool. Raven dipped a claw into the rapidly cooling water. The centre of the pool was still warm and he had a quick bath, enjoying the warmth as it soothed his aching muscles. Maybe his brother had the right idea, a warm bath at this time of year was good for the soul.

The happy family of raccoons gathering on the shore reset his thoughts. If he ever decided to try warming a tidal pool, he would have to be sure it was free of critters first. He sighed, there were so many things he could change to make his life more comfortable. Although, somehow, he didn't think Bilgat would approve.

The water was almost back to it's normal freezing temperature as Raven climbed out. A grateful raccoon was waiting and the thanks he received cheered Raven considerably.

About time I got some thanks and respect, he thought as he took to the sky.

His stomach grumbled, *how about a bit of respect for me?* it complained. So, with the hope that Bilgat had found some breakfast, he turned back, searching for the two eagles.

Not one, but two fish heads waited for him on the rocks at the foot of the high cliff. As he wolfed down the fish, he described his discovery of the hot pool to Bilgat and Farcry. When he repeated the raccoon's information that the white raven had created it, Farcry shook his head.

"I knew he was going to be trouble the minute I saw him on that beach," he muttered.

"I assume you didn't find any breakfast," remarked Bilgat, watching as Raven picked through the remains of the fish heads. For the first time that morning Raven grinned, "I admit, that hotpool sent all thoughts of breakfast from my mind.

Bilgat snorted in disbelief, "That's a first," he chuckled, and then added "Well Farcry here says your brother is holed up in an old boat shed at the end of the bay and he's apparently pretty sick."

Whilst Raven ate, Farcry retold the events of the last few days. From spotting the bedraggled mound of feathers washed up in the tide line, to the last few days of chaos as the white raven had stolen food, caused an accident, attacked a child and possibly killed a gull. He described the wavering, uncontrolled flight across the bay that ended in his hitting a piling and staggering into the shed.

Raven gulped down the last piece of fish and looked at Bilgat, "Then let's not waste time, I should check him out."

There was no movement on the docks at this early hour. No-one saw the trio glide over the boats and land, side by side, on a crossbar between two pilings at the end of the ramp. Curiosity sent Raven's eyes scanning the dilapidated buildings half sunk in the mud. A feeling of apprehension sent a shudder through his whole body. A slight movement in the end shed caught Raven's attention. Along with a strange tingling sensation at the base of his feathers on the top of his head, sending a wake-up call to the other half of his consciousness. Without giving his brain a chance to argue, Raven decided to investigate.

White Raven liked the old boat shed. He was out of sight of the village and it was fairly dry. Apart from the remains of a few swallow nests, some old crab pots and several rusty marine parts it was empty. From his perch on a beam he could see right down the bay, even though his vision was blurred and he was seeing double. Still, he could watch the comings and goings on the dock without moving his head. Not that he could at the moment, his whole body was numb and his head felt as if it was a huge, heavy rock sitting on his shoulders.

He looked hard at the two black birds coming toward him and scowled. There was a familiarity in the flight pattern and, as they came closer, four wings blended into two. He could see it was another raven. And not just any other raven, this one was as large as himself. This raven not only looked strong, he looked powerful. Each downward wing beat had strength in it that challenged the very wind. Yet there was a grace in his flight that only comes from confidence and well-being.

White Raven's scowl deepened. He didn't feel any well-being. He felt down right unwell-being. Several oily bits of brown still clung to him in places that he couldn't reach with his beak. The coolness of the night had hardened the largest clumps. Even with scraping himself against the centre beam, all he had managed to dislodge were a few lumps along with several feathers. Trouble was, some of the brown stuck to his beak had melted and plugged up his nostrils. He could smell it and taste it in the back of his throat; it made him dizzy.

The nauseous feeling added to the colossal headache he suffered from hitting the pylon. Now, another raven was flying into his shed, looking as if he owned the place. Well, he'd see about that!

His screech was not what it should have been and came out more a half strangled croak as the black raven landed.

"What do you want?" He snarled.

"Don't you recognize me, brother?"

White Raven squinted. His vision was far from normal and, although he could see the other bird was a raven, a damned arrogant raven at that, his red eyes still refused to focus on close objects and the other bird's features blurred.

Yet . . . something niggled at his drugged, befuddled brain. The voice was familiar. It sounded like . . . but it couldn't be . . . his great grandfather? This voice had power. This voice demanded respect. This bird had a strength he could feel. Yet this bird was too young. His memory of the past and that old dictatorial bird made him shudder and he squinted again. It couldn't be . . .

"Did you call me 'brother'? I'm not you're brother." White Raven sneered at Raven "My brother was a scrawny thing and probably died years ago, that's if he ever managed to fly from our birth-nest. Besides he had a huge bald spot on the top of his head and no tail feathers last time I saw him."

"I know."

"Oh you know, do you? Well maybe you also know that I don't like sharing my perch; especially with another raven." With a sudden burst of strength, he stepped toward Raven, puffing his chest out as much as he could, irritation fuelling his anger and overriding the pain in his joints. "So flap off and leave me alone. I've got enough problems without having to entertain the local idiot."

Raven eyed his brother carefully. It was obvious to him, whatever powers his brother had, the spirits did not endorse them or he would not be in this terrible state. Yet, if you could believe a racoon, he had created the hot spring, and, according to Farcry's message to Bilgat, he had escaped from some prison, turned a tidal pool into fresh water, had healed himself at least once, so why not now? He needed to know more.

"If you have a problem, maybe I can help."

It suddenly occurred to the white raven that he could use this pest to get rid of the brown from his tail feathers. He felt stronger as this other bird came closer. He could feel some of his strength returning. All he had to do was get rid of the poison. If he got this pest to remove it, it would most likely poison the aggravating nuisance. Kill two birds with one bite, so to speak, he sniggered to himself at his own morbid little joke, and, with considerably more friendliness, he turned to Raven.

"Well, since you asked, you could help me get this mud off my tail. We must have had rain in the night and one of the old swallow nests, or something, broke up, sending bits of mud everywhere. I seem to have strained my neck and can't reach back. It's causing my tail feathers to stick together and is very uncomfortable."

Raven knew he was lying, ravens never give in this easily. "I'll try, let me see."

White Raven lowered his head to hide the smirk, and Raven could see the length of his back.

What a mess, Raven thought. Unexpectedly the beam they were on shook, causing Raven to back up quickly. The white raven, already unsteady on his feet, almost fell in the water. He staggered back, flattening himself against the upright beam, as a sudden gust of wind whistled through the cobwebs.

"PSSSsssssss . . . on"

The breeze whispered close to Raven's ear.

"PSssssn"

It ruffled his feathers then drifted up through the rafters.

"What . . . the . . . ?" White Raven adjusted his grip and looked at his visitor, his eyes questioning.

"A small earth-shake I guess. No harm. Not unusual. You OK?" asked Raven. He sounded cheerful.

"I guess." White Raven muttered doubtfully. He hated cheerful.

"It seems to have settled down now. So where were we? Oh yes, your tail feathers. Why don't you turn around so I can see them properly?"

With a grunt and a shrug of his shoulders, the white raven shuffled around on the perch.

Raven could see the remains of the brown. Poison, the brown was poison, that's what the wind had said, well that explained his brother's red eyes and dazed state. It wasn't mud at all and his brother knew it. He had seen the crafty glint in the white bird's eye before he turned, which told Raven that his brother also knew it was poison and was expecting him to get sick as well.

He leaned forward, out of his brother's line of vision, and pecked at a couple of clean feathers that had somehow managed to escape the meltdown. As he did so he imagined the lump of brown on the closest feather to his beak exploding like a ripe seedpod. Avoiding the really bad feathers he pecked at the clean ones slowly moving across the base of White Raven's tail.

Making sure that the worst of the brown-coated feathers were left untouched, he pecked and preened the clean ones till he decided it was time to leave; before White Raven began to wonder why he wasn't feeling any better and his visitor wasn't getting sick. Besides he should get back to Bilgat and Farcry as, by the looks of it, it could be days before his brother would be recovered enough to be trouble again. Maybe by then, he would think of some way to trap or contain him, maybe forever.

"I don't feel so good," he croaked, as he teased at the last of the clean feathers. He coughed, doing his best to sound as if he was choking, then, letting his wings hang limp, he staggered away from the white raven.

"I need to get back to my own tree. Sorry it must be something I had for breakfast, I feel really dizzy." He gasped, realizing it wasn't far from the truth. He felt weak. Wether it was from the brown or the closeness of his brother, he didn't know. He stumbled on the beam and then, before White Raven had a chance to look at him too closely, he took off, feigning a jerky flight as he flapped his way over the docks.

Once he was behind the shed and out of the sight of any bird that may have been up in the rafters watching him, he straightened his flight and turned to cross the waters to the Douglas-fir where Bilgat and Farcry waited. The further he was from his brother the better he felt. Strange that being close to the poison should have such an strange effect on him.

"I heard," said Bilgat the minute he landed.

"I figured you would be listening in."

"He tried to kill you." Bilgat continued, indignation clear in his voice. "His mind's a mess, but that thought was loud and clear. We both heard it. He deliberately tried to kill you. By the way, he didn't believe you were his brother."

"Somehow I didn't think he would. I am surprised that the poison hasn't killed him. I was beginning to get sick just being close to him. What is it anyway?"

"It's a human-treat-food. Farcry called it 'brown'. It's highly poisonous, even the aroma it gives off makes you see strange things if inhaled too deeply."

A thought crossed Bilgat's mind and he looked closer

at Raven. "You OK? Didn't breath in too deep I hope."

"No, I'm OK. I think the local wind whispered a warning in my ear. Besides the stuff smelled odd when I got close, I guessed it wasn't really mud so I held my breath between pecks. Once I was out of that shed I felt much better."

Bilgat let out a big sigh of relief.

"Hold on a minute, did you say Farcry knew about this stuff?" Raven indignantly turned his accusing eyes on the old bird.

"I did." Said Farcry calmly, "and I told you about it first thing this morning."

"Not me you didn't. I don't read minds. That little bit of information was rather important don't you think?" Sarcasm dripped from his beak.

"You took off before we had a chance to talk to you this morning." Bilgat cut in, defending the old bird. Then, changing the subject he added, "So, what did you gain from flying into the bear's den? Talk about asking for trouble."

"Not much, except that the spirits are not helping him. At least not this time." Raven still scowled at Farcry, "I don't know how he changed the other things that Farcry saw or the hotpool, but he certainly hasn't found a way to help himself this time."

"Maybe the brown has affected his brain so that he can't," reasoned Farcry.

"Maybe." Said Bilgat, thoughtfully, "If so we need to think of some way to stop him whilst he is still under the influence."

Raven turned to Bilgat and nodded. "My thinking exactly."

The White Raven   159

17
The Power of Copper

A simple question. "If it's poison, how come people don't get sick from it?" Asked Raven.

Bilgat tipped his head and looked at his companion. "You could ask why, when they suck on those firesticks of theirs and blow out smoke, they don't burn up? Their bodies are larger and far different on the outside to ours, so who knows what's on the inside."

Raven nodded, the events of the morning replayed through his head. He needed to know more about the area, if he was to come up with a solution that would contain the problem raven. Farcry was still disappointed that only the two of them had responded to his call and that there was no other regiment or flight squadrons on the horizon. Even though Raven had told them he had corrected the hotpool, no assurances from Bilgat that Raven would be able to handle things, appeased his concern.

"I'm still wondering why he doesn't get rid of the brown the same way he cleaned himself up on the beach." Raven voiced his thoughts out loud.

"Maybe he doesn't know he can. We went over this before, you didn't know how you changed things at first." Commented Bilgat.

"I think that your idea of the brown affecting his ability to reason clearly, has a lot to do with it," added Farcry.

"Raven, you know how these things worked for you, better than anyone," pointed out Bilgat.

"Yeah, well nothing worked for me till I saved that frog. I sincerely doubt I could have pulled off any of the changes that my brother seems to have accomplished without help. Either he is a lot stronger than I am or spirits are helping him too."

Farcry shook his head, "Surely not, it was the spirits that banished him in the first place."

"Soo . . . where were they when he escaped? Tell me that. They obviously screwed up there, so maybe they screwed up again. Not being of this earth I think they are out of touch with reality. "

There was ripple in the ozone layer high above the Douglas-fir where the trio perched.

Raven's disrespect for the spirits shocked Farcry.

Bilgat had a hard time not laughing at the look on the old eagle's face. Smothering his urge to chuckle he said, "Apart from changing the pool into hotwater, he really hasn't done any more of those fancy transformations since he arrived at the bay. Honestly, all he has really done is steal and cause havoc. He must be using his own inner strength. Grandfather always said we all have the ability to change things, especially ourselves. We just have to believe."

"Now you're starting to sound like your grandfather," said Raven, "preaching the word of the wing. Believe in what? The spirits? Give me the sun, the sky, the wind and the air we breathe, that's what I believe in."

Then, seeing the look on the faces of the two eagles he toned it down a little.

"I'm not saying there aren't spirits floating around out there, just that, if you eagles expect everyone to believe in them, then everyone will wait, praying for the spirits to change things; which they won't, and then nothing gets done."

Another ripple in the ozone layer. The truth hurts.

"Well, that white raven must have done something to the sun, and I can't see the spirits helping him with that." Said Farcry, only ever so slightly mollified. "It's pretty odd that it's been sunny and warm from the day he arrived until today when he is sick. It's the first time I've seen the fog in days, not even first thing in the morning. That's totally unheard of in these parts, especially this time of year."

"Well, wherever he was getting his strength from, Raven sais he's weak now and unable to fight back, so we strike whilst we have the advantage." Bilgat chipped in.

"There you go again, thinking like an eagle" said Raven. "What do you want me to do . . . kill him? Turn him into a chickadee? Oh, Oh, how about an earthworm? He's my brother and somehow I suspect if he was created greedy and selfish then he won't change. He is the way he is. It's like I'm good and he's bad. If the spirits are involved, as you say, then have you thought of what might happen to me if he was killed and his spirit allowed to escape his body."

"What?" Said Bilgat with sudden interest.

"I don't KNOW," snapped Raven," that's the point. I don't know how these spirits created us in the first place; I don't really know how they manage to change things, or if they really do. I just know I can change things. Maybe it's with their help or maybe it's from something else, like my own inner strength, who knows? No, we can't take the risk of killing him. I have to find another way to confine him, and quickly, before the brown all wears off. If can he call up fire from the middle earth to heat the water in that creek, who knows what he will do next. He could have killed all the sea life in the inlet not to mention the returning salmon this fall."

"Could we ask the people of the village to help, perhaps?" Asked Farcry, "I think the're quite angry with him and would like to be rid of him as much as us."

Raven looked hard at the old eagle.

"And how are we supposed to do that? Did Bilgat tell you about the river?" He asked sharply, looking from one eagle to the other, his feathers on the top of his head stiffening.

Bilgat shook his head. "No Raven, I didn't."

"Hmmm," slightly mollified, the raven's feathers relaxed. "Well that was an odd choice of words. What do you know about the people in this town? Is there someone who could catch a bird?"

"There is this farmhouse in on the outskirts of town that has cages for injured animals. It's owned by an old man who's wife passed away a few years back. He misses her." Farcry's voice wavered, as thoughts of his own mate surfaced. He shook his head and continued, "Sometimes he takes in birds too. I did see an owl with a broken wing in one of his cages, as well as one of our own young eaglets that had fallen from its nest. The old man raised him, but the youngster changed. He lost his wild and couldn't even talk our language let alone mindspeak.

"So we need to get this man to catch and cage my brother over there. Let's go. The longer we delay, the more chance that he will recover."

"You have a plan?" The old eagle, looked respectfully at Raven and breathed a great sigh of relief.

"Not exactly but I'm working on it. Let's see these cages and we'll go from there."

Farcry looked across the branch at the grandson of the great eagle. The look of askance on his face and the questions that were probing Bilgat's head were quite comical to the younger bird.

"Don't ask," he replied with a chuckle, "just come along for the flight. If I know anything about anything, this one will probably be as interesting as our last adventure.

Raven thought hard as the trio flew across the bay. The last time he had spoken to a human he had transformed himself and pretended to be a kayaker. The west coast of this large island was rugged and, during the last few days, he had not seen a single kayak. If he needed to speak to the old man that Farcry was talking about, what excuse could he come up with for being a stranger in town? Kayaking was out of the question. But a traveler needed a mode of transportation; he could hardly say he flew. Maybe, if he could find one of those metal boxes, he could drive into town as a sightseer, but what reason could he devise to encourage them to capture the white raven?

Maybe he could say he was attacked.

While his brother was holed up in that old shed, he was accessible, but how would a visitor know he was there? He could say he saw him fly in there, but what excuse could he come up with for hanging around the sheds in the first place?

Hmmmm, Farcry said the man rescued animals. Better to say he had seen a sick bird that needed help.

People used boxes to take photos of birds. Whatever a photo was, he had no idea. Back home people had wanted to take photos of Bilgat. They had called them shots. He assumed it was some kind of recording device that remembered a scene or person. Maybe he could say he was using his photo box when he saw the sick white raven.

That might work. He reworked the thoughts in his head and was so immersed in his plans that he lost track of where they were. He wasn't hungry or his stomach would have alerted him to the fact they were flying over the local garbage dump, Raven's favourite free food store.

A clutter of metal scraps caught his eye and his thoughts again returned to the transportation problem. His eyes searched the surrounding area as they flew and spotted a couple of old cars in varying states of decay. Several of their parts were scattered around, some half covered in weeds and brambles, others almost completely buried in garbage bags and wood chips from a local mill, that were being used to bury the mess. Nothing looked suitable until he spotted an unusual looking shape tucked behind a small stand of trees. Most of the body was still covered in what had once been some sort of material but it had deteriorated so badly that the front of the vehicle was now sticking out. The holes in the rest of the fabric were so ripped and torn that even from this height Raven could see the car had no roof: a bonus for a bird that likes to feel the wind.

"How much further," he asked as he memorized the spot, noting the car was actually quite close to the road.

"We're almost there," said Farcry. "See the hollow

coming up between those tall pines? It's the site of an old copper mine. The steep sides form a crater and walls for some of the pens of the larger animals.

As they flew closer, the land dropped away and an old farm house with it's barns came into view. Behind one they could see cages that were quite large, some as tall as the barn itself. They flew closer and Raven realized there were birds in some of the cages. His anger flared and he was about to fly down to take a closer look when Bilgat screeched right in his ear.

"Raven, NO."

Farcry, who was wheezing a bit in an effort to keep ahead as he guided the younger birds, managed to gasp out, "They are all unable to fly."

Bilgat nodded in the direction of an old snag that had several large eagles on it.

"They aren't in cages," he pointed out, "but they couldn't leave even if they wanted too, they all have damaged wings. For many different reasons all these birds were dying. They have been rescued by the humans and made well again. But some are no longer able to hunt for food so they are caged and fed. The cages are meant to protect them, not restrain them. If you open all the cages they will only return in time for their next meal or die. They have no place to go. This is their home now and only hope."

Raven scowled down at the pens.

"I'd rather be dead." He mumbled. "Especially as I'm now deaf in one ear. Look, they even have a couple of ravens down there."

"They do release birds if they recover," assured Farcry.

"So if they bring my brother out here, will they give him a dose of medicine and then release him again? What good is that?"

"Not always, Raven. See that large paddock with a high wire fence? Look closer at the shadows under that group of trees near that big rock. See the bear? He wandered into town a few years back and took such a liking to the people food he found in the garbage back there at the dump, he started raiding the gardens and doing a lot of damage. The people trapped him and took him up into the hills but in less that three moon cycles he was back. He now has his own small range and gets fed daily. He's happy and so are the people."

Raven snorted. "That's typical. Damn lazy bear. Haven't met one yet that's not always looking for a free meal."

Bilgat looked sharply at Raven, a question clear on his face, he opened his beak and then decided against it.

"What???" Snapped Raven.

"Nothing."

"Well if you've finished with the tour then I need to go back to the dump. Some of us have work to do."

With that he turned abruptly and flew back toward the dump and the old car.

"I heard what you were thinking," chuckled Farcry, his voice in a whisper and his old eyes glistening with moisture. Bilgat couldn't tell if it was from the effort of flying or whether it was laughter.

"Yes, well it's not the first time he's overlooked his own failings. I doubt it will be the last," said Bilgat as they turned and let the wind carry them aloft. Then he added, " I wonder what he has in mind and what on earth he wants back at the dump. I hope it's not more rotten food."

18
The car

The old car was content to just rust away. She didn't see the raven land in the bushes close to her hood. She had retired many moons ago and enjoyed each day as they came and went. Last spring a small field mouse had made a nest inside one of her back cushions, gaining entry through a big rip in the cover of the rumble seat. When the youngsters played tag across her dashboard, she felt her life was complete. Rabbits hid behind her wheels when the eagles and hawks were flying overhead, and little bugs and beetles found homes under her carpeting. Her engine had long been removed, which had lifted a huge weight off her old frame, and a common garden variety of creeper had wrapped itself around the perished mounting blocks. They were all her friends.

Her first clue that things were not quite right was the itchy sandpaper feeling that ran over her entire body, followed by that scrubbed clean sensation that you get after one of those automatic car washes has spat you out. She had tried to forget those fearful few seconds when she wondered if all that water had fouled up her plugs and she wouldn't be able to start. But what was she thinking? She didn't have any spark plugs. Not any more, and she wasn't coming out of a carwash. She had only seconds to realize that the old tarp that was keeping her tailpipe nice and warm all these years had vanished, before the vibration in her frame registered the fact that she was moving.

Floating would be more to the point, just a discernible fraction of an inch above the ground. She tried her best to turn her wheels but they met no resistance and just spun in mid air. As the car emerged from the bushes, it looked like it's wheels were actually moving over the ground. The strange thing was, it moved silently, just a few crackle and snaps from the surrounding branches and swishing of the tall grass.

If the old car could have seen herself, she would have been shocked. So shocked that, if she did still have an engine, it would have seized. She shone with a new paint job, jet black; new interior, also jet-black, and her chrome sparkled. Raven loved sparklies. The old car glittered and shone as bright as the day she had come off the production line. Perched, grinning cheekily, on top of her steering wheel was a large black raven looking remarkably like an out-of-place hood ornament.

Without hesitation Farcry, flew in and landed on the back of the drivers seat. All thoughts of decorum vanished; he was a yearling again.

"How fast can you make it go?" He asked, his eyes alight with excitement. "This transformation stuff you do is fun."

Bilgat circled nervously overhead his eyes watching the road.

"What if another car comes along?" He screeched down at the two joy riders. "How will you explain two birds driving a man machine?"

"I'll deal with it when the time comes, and, by the way, it's a sports car. This one is apparently called '32 Ford Roadster."

"How do you know? Who told you?"

"The car."

Raven's reply stunned Bilgat, but only for a moment. "You talked to a car?"

"Yea', well '32 here isn't just any old car. Just because it's a chunk of metal doesn't mean it doesn't have feelings you know."

'Feelings! It's just a machine, which, by the way, doesn't make any noise. The'll be questions if you drive up to the farmhouse door in that."

"Then I won't. I'll park her at the top of the ridge where it's visible and walk in."

"Her! Did you say 'her'? How can you tell?"

Raven ignored Bilgat and turned his attention to Farcry who was happily turning all the knobs on the dashboard with his beak.

"Can I sit on the steering wheel whilst you're gone?" He asked hopefully.

Overhead, Bilgat groaned.

"Sure," said Raven still ignoring the exasperated splutters from above, "and I think we are here."

They rounded a curve in the track. In front of them was a large, closed gate.

"Well that settles the question of driving up to the front door," he muttered to himself as he pulled off the road onto the grassy verge.

With relief, the old roadster felt the ground beneath her wheels again as she sank down into the grass. She relaxed. Bewildered, confused and, being extremely tired from trying to get a grip on herself, she dozed off almost immediately.

Raven hopped down from the top of the steering wheel to the seat. Not waiting for Raven to change his mind, Farcry leapt up to take his place. He bounced up and down, his talons gripping the wheel cover as he peered through the windscreen. It was a few moments before he realized that there was a young man now sitting behind him in the car.

Shrieking in surprise and fear, he leapt up into the

sky, catching his tail feathers on the mirror attached to the windshield. Bilgat, still circling above the ridge, smirked as the old bird flew up to join him.

"It's just Raven," he croaked, "I tried to warn you. If you hadn't been so immersed with the workings of the car, you'ld have seen him transform. Quite interesting. See he's getting out of the car. Ooops he hasn't got his balance yet. Oh there he goes, he's got the hang of it. He says the first step is the worst. He always wants to hop. Must feel weird with all that cloth wrapped around you instead of feathers."

The old eagle looked down at Raven. Shock and fascination are such a strange combination of emotions that all Farcry could do was stare. The youth below him bore no resemblance to a bird. The only hint that it was, in fact, Raven was the jet black hair that glistened with blue and purple highlights, just like the feathers on a raven's back. The black jeans and jacket only added to the picture.

Raven stretched himself. The change was getting easier each time he did it. He was getting used to the strange restrictive feel of the clothes on his back. Getting out of the car had proved interesting. Looking back at the closed car door he realized he should have done his transformation outside of the car.

Arms had replaced wings and the fingers at the end of each arm were so much more useful than talons. When he ran his fingers over the door handle, it had felt smooth to the touch and fit neatly into the palm of his hand. A small twist and the door had opened. It would have taken him ages to master that using his feet. He grinned to himself and flexed his fingers. I figured out how to open the door, he thought, pleased with himself. Yes, I'm getting much better at this.

He looked up at the two eagles flying overhead;

how small they seemed.

Now it was up to him. He would have to go down to the farm and talk to the old man.

The gate was easy to open, it just needed a good push. The hinges creaked as Raven swung it back, and several of the birds in the cages started screeching, but there was no sign of human life in the buildings below.

Well, best get it over with, he thought and started walking down the lane. His stride was a bit jerky at first, the downhill slope didn't help, but he soon got used to it. Just when he began to feel confident in his walking abilities, he felt a draining wave of weakness go through him. A few more steps and it came again, stronger, up from the ground through the soles of his shoes, his feet, up his legs into his body. He faltered in mid stride. Another step and his knees folded underneath him. In seconds he found himself lying flat on the ground in the middle of the dusty road.

He tried to get up and realized his feathers were back; he was a bird again. He felt strange, a tremor ripple through him, the road was warm but he felt cold and shivered.

"What happened?" A concerned Bilgat landed on the road beside him. His bright yellow beak poked within inches of Raven's face.

"Dunno," Raven groaned, "but I feel awful. I don't think I can get back up to the car by myself. I can hardly lift my wings."

A raven, with his wing feathers spread across the backs of two eagles, was a sight for the records. Bilgat and Farcry helped Raven back up the track, through the gate, to the waiting car.

The further out of the crater they hopped the better Raven began to feel, until finally, when they set him down by the car, he was his old self again.

The White Raven

"Thanks guys . . . never thought I would need a lift from an eagle and here I had two. I'm feeling much better."

"Thank . . . good . . . ness . . . for . . . that." gasped Farcry as he slumped down on the grass. "You're heavy and I really don't think I could have carried you another step."

If Raven was a different bird he would have felt a twinge of guilt. After all, he had known that his strength had returned quite a ways back down the track, but to have not one but two eagles carrying you as if you were a king: was an experience not likely to repeat itself. Once he had started to feel more himself, he had reveled in the luxury. But then, a raven is a raven and guilt does not exist in a raven's vocabulary.

"So what was that all about?" asked Bilgat. "You collapsed and changed back faster than I could blink my eye. If that had happened in town with people around you, you would have been in real trouble. We certainly couldn't have rescued you then.

Raven just shook his head; he didn't know what to think.

Farcry's breathing had slowed to normal and, seeing the worried look in Raven's eyes, asked, "Did you feel anything before you collapsed."

"Well," Raven thought back, "not much, just a sudden draining of strength. I ignored it at first; everything in that human body felt strange. Then I began to feel heavy. It was as if the land wanted to swallow me up. It seemed to be sucking all my strength out through the soles of my shoes. It got worse with each step, then everything happened so fast I didn't have a chance to think."

"Hmmm," murmured Bilgat, "You were about halfway down the side of the hill. Maybe you walked over a force line. Grandfather often spoke of special places where the life forces are the strongest. Can't say I really knew what he meant"

"Oh here we go again with the spiritual stuff," snarled Raven, "If that's the case then it's a negative force because it just about sucked the life out of me."

"Heh, it's not a bad idea you know," said Bilgat defensively, not wanting to give up the argument. "You were entering an old copper mine. Maybe you are affected by copper. Maybe it drained your power. It was always important to the ancients, and now-a-days humans use it to make copper wire. Grandfather sais they send power through it to light up their homes. It didn't affect Farcry and I but we are eagles, we don't have any powers. Think about it, it didn't kill you, just stole your strength."

Deep in thought, Raven looked back down into the old, man-made crater, his curiosity aroused. He hated to admit it, but Bilgat could be right.

"Copper. You really think that might have been it? Good job I didn't take the car down after all. That really would have created a problem. Well there's only one way to test your theory." He flew up on to the top of the gatepost. "I have to go down there again."

Hearing a gasp from Farcry and seeing the look of concern on Bilgat's face, he reassured them.

"Don't worry, you won't have to carry me back. I know what to expect now and I'll stop the instant I feel the pull. We'll soon find out if it's the copper."

He hopped down from the post and started down the road. He hadn't gone very far before he felt the first pull. He stopped, flapped a few feet to the other side of the road and tried again. There, it was a definite downward tug. He backed up and flew several yards around the crater and tried again with the same results. The almost circular open pit was about a mile across, so it took the raven some time to test it selecting random spots around the rim. All with the same result; the further into the crater he went, the weaker he felt.

Finally he flew back to the waiting eagles. "Well that blows that idea. I can't get down there to speak to the old man, so we will have to come up with another plan."

"I've been thinking about that. I've seen a young girl visit him a lot, probably his daughter. I know where she works in town." Piped up Farcry. "Can we can talk to her."

"We! What's with the we?"

'Sorry Raven, it's just a figure of speech."

"Not a bad idea though," added Bilgat. "Raven gets along really well with the human females. They like him." He leaned closer to Farcry and whispered. "And I think he likes them."

"I heard that," said Raven, scowling at his comrade in flight, who was enjoying his embarrassment. Turning to Farcry he asked. "Exactly where in town?"

"Down at the docks. I've seen her go into a building just inside the gates."

The thought of driving the car all the way into town cheered raven considerably. "Right then, let's head back into town, we've wasted enough time here. I'll check out the daughter and maybe I can convince her to capture my brother. If her or her father manage to get him into a cage, and take him out to that farmhouse, he will be so weakened by the copper he will never be able to fly out of there, even if they do let him go. Whatever strength or power he has, down there he will definitely lose it."

With those cheerful thoughts in mind, Raven maneuvered the car back out on to the road, even Bilgat relaxed enough to join Farcry perched on the top of the rumble seat.

They were about a mile from the main road into town, before Bilgat started to get nervous again. His sixth sense began to warn him of incoming danger. Sure enough, as the old car rounded the next bend in the gravel road, his sharp eyes spotted a cloud of dust on the road ahead.

"Incoming car," he screeched at Raven, who was enjoying the wind blowing through his feathers as he perched on top of the steering wheel.

Raven's reaction was swift. In seconds all signs of claws and feathers had vanished and, in their place, hands belonging to a young man gripped the steering wheel, his jet-black hair ruffled by the breeze as the car continued forward. The cloud of dust came closer and, in its midst was an old farm truck. Behind the wheel was an elderly man who waved at Raven as he passed.

Raven waved back.

As the truck vanished around the bend behind them, the two eagles, both of whom had hopped down to the floor of the car, peered out again.

"You know something," said Bilgat, studying the road behind them, "we're not making any dust."

Farcry looked back at the slowly settling dust from the old farm truck.

"We're not leaving any tracks either," he added, "I reckon that was the old man from the farm, I wonder how far he will get before he realizes it."

Raven interrupted them. "Don't worry, humans today rarely notice little things like that, especially as they get older. Still before we get into town perhaps we should make contact with the road."

The jolting as the wheels hit the potholes was unsettling after the previous smooth ride, and the birds were relieved when they saw a junction ahead.

"This looks like the main road." Said Raven. "Which way do you think? I seem to have lost my sense of direction, traveling this low to the ground."

"Turn toward the sun," said Farcry, as the car slowed.

Checking to make sure it was free of traffic, Raven maneuvered the old automobile onto the paved road.

"It's not far now," added Farcry, "In fact, just round the next bend, then over a ridge and you are at the outskirts of the town.

"Then it's time we left," said Bilgat. "Come on Farcry, before another car shows up."

With that he leapt into the air letting the slipstream of the car give him an extra lift. He was followed by a reluctant Farcry.

Not a minute too soon either, as a noisy truck rounded the bend in front of them. At the same time a car pulled out of a side road and started following the roadster. Raven felt a bit nervous with another vehicle following so closely and was surprised to have the steering wheel jerked out of his grip. The car swung over to the right hand side of the road.

"Don't you know how to drive?" A grinding steel-scraping-whisper emitted itself from beneath the floorboards of the old car. "There are rules you know. You want to put me back in that junkyard? You want to get killed? Do you even have a license to drive?"

"Rules, what rules?"

Raven hadn't realized that the driving of a car had rules. Another vehicle joined them on the road. If Raven had expected to make a quiet, uneventful trip into the town, he had chosen the wrong car. The heads of the passers-by were turning to watch as the shiny, beautifully restored, antique car drove down the hill.

"You had better leave the driving up to me," grumbled the old car. "Good job I know where I am, I used to travel this road every day."

Raven was more than a little annoyed at having to give up control of the car, he scowled as they came to a stop in front of a set of lights.

"I didn't tell you to stop," he snapped.

"No, you didn't but the lights did," smirked the car. "Red means stop and green means go."

Raven squinted up at the lights. "Which one's red?" He asked, just as the top light went out and the bottom one came on.

The old car rumbled forward ignoring his question and Raven realized that there was now a distinct rumble coming from beneath the metal. It sounded like the snoring of an old bear. They were nearing the centre of town but Raven was more concerned with getting back control of the car than worrying about where they were.

"I gave you life." He yelled over the growl coming from under the hood.

"And I'm saving yours," grated the car.

"I can stop all this right now."

There was a gurgle from somewhere among the metal that sounded like water in rusty pipes.

"Look around you, and rethink that decision. A fine state we would be in if I stopped dead in all this traffic."

Raven looked around and realized the car was right. They were driving down Main Street and there was nowhere to go but forward.

"So, where are you going?" Asked Raven through gritted teeth.

"To the office."

"And where's that?"

The old car hesitated and seemed uncertain for the first time since she had taken control.

"I . . . I'm not sure," she spluttered. "The building used to be right here on Main Street, but I don't see it. My parking spot is gone and the road patterns have changed."

"So you're lost?"

"No, I'm not LOST." She snapped back at him, "Just a little disoriented. It's been many moons since I was in town. I guess the old building has been torn down and replaced. It was getting old, like my driver." Her voice began to quiver and the car started to tremble. "Nothing is the same, it's all changed."

She sounded as if she was starting to panic, the smooth ride was becoming jerky and unknown loose parts were beginning to rattle.

"Do you know where the main docks are?" Raven demanded.

"Ye . . . ees, I think so. They used to be left at the end of this street, and down the hill, just past the filling station.

"Then head there and find somewhere to stop."

"It's called 'park'," muttered the old car as she tried to re-gain some of her dignity.

"What is? The dock? Are you saying the dock is a park?"

"No. It's called 'Parking'. You don't just stop a car, you park it." The old car seemed to have re-established control of herself and slowed, as it came to the end of Main street.

"Stick your left arm out," she growled.

"Huh?"

"Don't ask, just do it. You need to let the driver behind you know we are going to turn left. That's called signaling."

"Oh." Raven took his left hand off the wheel and stuck his arm over the side of the car.

"Not like that. Stick it out straight, if it hangs down the car behind will get the wrong message and think you're going to stop."

Raven stuck his arm out straight, resenting the fact that he was unable to do anything but follow the car's instructions. He was more than glad Bilgat wasn't sitting beside him enjoying his discomfort.

They had hardly gone more than half a block when the old car slowed again. The side of the road in this part of town was clear of cars and, with a graceful turn of her wheels, the '32 roadster pulled in tight against the curb and stopped.

Raven let out a huge sigh of relief. The road continued down hill for a short way, and at the bottom, was a large gate. Just inside that was the building that Farcry had described.

Raven stepped out of the car. He looked up at the weak effort put out by the sun, almost mid-day and his stomach was rumbling again. Doing his best to put the thought of food behind him, he took a deep breath to steady himself, then set off down the hill.

19
Lunch

Never argue with a kingfisher, you won't win.
Especially a female belted kingfisher; they are the
worst. One of the more colourful shore birds in British
Columbia, the belted kingfisher makes it's home up
and down the coast. It's not only the brightly coloured
plumage that distinguishes this bird, it is also the bird's
call which is more of a coarse cackle, resembling a
laugh. One of the interesting things about this bird is
that it is only the female that has the bright orange belt
around her middle. The male has a plain white and grey
chest.

Unfortunately for White Raven, the old shed was one of the prized fishing spots for a certain, especially noisy, female kingfisher. Small fish gather in the shadows and, as the late morning sun threw long beams of light into the shed, the kingfisher liked to sit in the rafters watching for the light to bounce off a silver back.

Her favourite perch happened to also be the middle of the shed. The sun was weak; the morning fog had not left the bay yet, and the overhead haze filtered out what little warmth there was. Still, even on rainy days, she had caught some fair size piling perch under these old beams.

To find her favourite spot occupied by a large, dirty, white bird annoyed her to no end. It wasn't as if he was fishing. He was just sitting there huddled into a rather messy looking heap of scruffy, unpreened feathers.

Another thing about kingfishers is that they are seldom polite and have an annoying habit of speaking their mind.

"That's my fishing spot you're lazing in." She screeched down from one of the crossbeams. "If you're not fishing, then move over. Go into the corner over there if you want to sleep. Just get out of my way."

White Raven stirred himself. The cackle of the kingfisher penetrated through the dark cloud that had made a permanent home in head.

His red eyes turned in her direction. His befuddled brain made out the shapes of two small birds with very large beaks. They kept hovering, side by side above him and then blurred into one.

"MOVE."

The kingfisher wasn't the slightest bit disturbed by the red eyes glaring back at her. Lots of birds have red eyes, including her old friend Loony. The spiked feathers were a bit odd, but all seabirds feathers were spiky after being in the water, until they dried.

For once in his life the white raven had no strength to fight back. The screeching voice was annoying and all he wanted to do was get away from it. He shuffled along the beam until he reached the far side of the shed and worked his way into a back corner. There he found the cranky little bird had done him a favour. He could wedge himself between the two walls, which took some of the strain off his muscles. He relaxed and let the fuzziness take him into a restful stupor.

Two eagles flew high above the town, watching Raven as he strolled through the open gates and walked up the front steps of the Marina Office building. He had just reached the top step when the door burst open and a young girl stepped out. Seeing the young man standing in front of her, she hesitated.

"If you're looking for moorage you can take any spot on the main finger. Sorry but we are closed now for

---

lunch. I'll come down later to collect the fees."

Then, noticing Raven's startled expression, she added, "If that's all right with you."

"Well, actually, I came to find the girl whose father looks after sick birds and animals."

"Oh, well then you've found her, that's me. I'm Linda Kane, you're looking for George, my father, he's the animal protection officer for the district. What can I do for you?

"Well I wanted to report a sick white raven."

"A white raven? THE white raven. The one that's been driving everyone in town crazy?" Anger was evident in her voice. "That thief has been a real nuisance around town this past week. Don't know where he came from but there are more than a few people that would like to see the back of him, including me. He stole donuts I had just bought as a treat for dad's birthday. Swooped down and stole them right off the roof of my car. I heard he also stole the Easter eggs from the park yesterday too and attacked a kid while he was at it."

"Well, maybe it was those eggs, but whatever it was, something has made him very sick, and he's holed up in the boat sheds down there on the old part of the docks." Then he added for good measure. "He looks as if he is almost dead."

"Well good riddance."

Then, realizing she was being petty, Linda looked closer at Raven. "You're new in town, what were you doing down on those old docks, they're not safe. Didn't you see the notice? If you fall in, the city won't be held responsible."

"Can't say I did. Sorry. I just wanted to take some pictures of the old sheds."

"Pictures? Are you a photographer?" Hardly waiting for his nod she continued on. "Well that explains it.

Even if you had seen the sign, you would have ignored it. Anything for the perfect shot, eh? Dad's quite a buff, still uses his old Nikon with black and white film. Develops his own. None of those new digitals for him."

Linda admired the attractive young man standing before her on the steps.

"Look, what did you say your name was? I'm starving and I'm about to go for a bite to eat. Want to come along? We don't get many visitors in town this time of year. My treat. You can tell me all about this bird over a sandwich. Come on, there's a coffee shop just around the corner."

"Ah, actually I didn't say my name but you can call me Ray, and lunch would be great. I haven't eaten for a while and, now that you mention it, I'm quite hungry."

"Well follow me then." With that, Linda turned the key in the lock and walked down the steps, guiding the way round the corner of the building to a brightly lit trailer that was tucked in between a couple of storage sheds.

Raven followed and, glancing toward the sky, he nodded. Linda's back was turned or she would have been very curious as to why he seemed to be sending some sort of message to the two eagles souring high above.

Bilgat and Farcry circled for several minutes after Raven vanished into the building.

"Now what?" said Farcry.

"Well, we could wait, but I think we should go and check out the white raven. It's been a while and I want to be sure he's still in the shed."

"You're right of course, and I wouldn't mind getting a closer look at him too."

The two birds flew down the docks and landed on a couple of old, weather-beaten pilings. From their perches they could see into the old building. At first Bilgat thought White Raven had indeed flown. He wasn't on the centre cross beam as Raven had described. Then his sharp eyes spotted the huddled clump of grubby, white feathers huddled in the back corner. He breathed a sigh of relief. On the shore, opposite the sheds, was a twisted arbutus tree. Without any verbal communication both birds agreed it would be a perfect spot to keep watch. If White Raven so much as moved a feather from that shed, Bilgat and Farcry would know.

In the boat shed, White Raven slept. What little warmth there was, radiating from the sun as it rose in the sky, penetrated the wood siding. Along with his own body heat, the warmth began to melt the remaining chocolate that clung to his feathers. It dripped onto the narrow walkway that went around the inside of the old building and congealed into a messy, glittery lump. It was almost noon when a couple of noisy barn swallows, looking for a nesting site, woke the white raven.

Disoriented, he struggled to remember where he was and why. As memories crept back into his brain, so did anger and resentment. His head hurt. He could tell from the throbbing that he had a bad bruise from where his head had made contact with the piling.

He lifted one wing. It felt as though each feather was made of wood; stiff and heavy. Some remnants of the brown still clung to the tips of his pinions and he did his best to shake them off. The effort almost unseated him from his perch, but, as each piece of brown dripped to the floor, he could feel a fraction of his strength return.

His anger and frustration reached a fever pitch, and still more brown melted.

As the dark cloud gradually dissipated from his brain,

thoughts of revenge filled the space.

It was warm inside the coffee shop and Raven felt the need to get rid of some of his clothing. Not knowing how to unfasten his jacket he did his best to ignore the trickle of water that ran down the back of his neck. Linda waved to the lady behind the counter.

"Two today Mary, on my tab. How about a couple of your salmon specials?" She turned to Raven "You do like salmon don't you?"

Raven nodded his head. "Who doesn't," he replied.

"What would you like to drink? Coffee, tea, bottle of water?"

Raven's last experience with a cup hadn't been that great.

"Water will be fine," he said. Thinking to himself that a bottle would be easier to handle.

"Then let's sit down, Mary will bring them out soon."

Linda slid into a booth beside a collection of black and white photos that hung on the wall above the table.

"See the pictures?" She said, "Dad took those. Pretty good don't you think?"

With her eyes focused on the pictures, she didn't notice as Raven, unused to bending his knees and sliding on a bench seat, stumbled as he got his legs crossed under the table. Although his toes were throbbing from having trodden on his own foot, Raven forced himself to look up at the wall.

The images were close-up photos of an eagle's head, with eyes that glared straight out of the picture right at the viewer. Even in black and white, the eyes were piercing.

Typical, thought Raven, everyone photographs eagles.

"Nice." He did his best to show enthusiasm. "Good contrast. That white raven should photograph well too."

"Right, the raven. In the old boat shed you said. Sick. Probably tried to eat the chocolate eggs. Chocolate is poison to a lot of animals you know, especially birds."

"I'm not sure if he actually ate it, but there is brown all over his feathers, especially his chest. It looks as if he fell in a mud puddle."

"The chocolate must have melted." Linda shook her head. "Wonder how that happened, maybe he laid on top of them, or maybe the sun melted them. It has been unseasonably hot lately. Who knows? Serves him right though." She added with some conviction. "Can't say I'm sorry for him."

"Well if he's that much of a pest, then now is the time to catch him and cage him up for good," pointed out Raven, hopefully.

"You're right, I'll call Dad, maybe he can bring a cage into town."

With that, she reached into her pocket and pulled out one of the talking boxes that Raven had seen humans use before. He had told Bilgat about them and was surprised to learn it was the human way of sending messages to other humans. Linda pushed a few buttons and in moments was talking; a strange disjointed kind of conversation.

". . . Ok, in about twenty minutes then . . . . . . Yes I'll be at the coffee shop . . . . . . OK Dad, the sooner we can get him caged the better . . . . . . OK see you soon, bye."

Raven did his best not to grin at her comment on getting his brother caged as soon as possible. My feelings exactly, he thought.

While she was talking, Raven's eyes returned to the pictures on the wall. The eagle in them looked a lot like Farcry. The penetrating eyes, the small scar on the side of his beak; only this bird was much younger. The feathers on it's head were a pristine white, not yellowed with age.

"There were a pair of eagles nesting at the mouth of the inlet," said Linda, following his gaze. "They were there for years. Haven't been back for two years now. I guess one of them died."

The sandwiches arrived along with a hot steaming mug of coffee and a bottle of water.

Raven studied his meal. Saliva filled his mouth. The sandwich looked easy to handle, but the bottle of water was confusing.

Linda turned back toward the table.

"Just enough time for lunch. Don't wait for me to start. Tuck in . . . Dad just got home and he's going to grab a cage and his medicine bag and meet us here. We've got about twenty minutes to finish this before he shows up. Then you can show us exactly where you saw that white menace."

She picked up the sandwich from her plate and bit into it.

"Thanks for the lunch," said Raven following her lead.

The salmon was chopped up, mixed with something to make it soft and had green bits in it. It tasted quite different and it was a few minutes before he realized it wasn't raw.

Hmmm, he thought, people sure know how to ruin the flavour of a perfectly good fish. Don't think Bilgat would like this one.

Linda was studying him.

"Don't you like it?" She asked.

"It's great," Raven lied with practised ease, one of the many things that Raven could do really well. "It's . . . ah . . . unusual, that's all, and quite different."

He took another bite and smiled as he concentrated

---

on the flavour of the bread rather than the mush that was in the middle of the two slices.

"Yes," he said, "quite different, and the bread is the best I've ever tasted,"

"Oh, Mary bakes her own, fresh everyday."

"Well thank you again, it's been a treat."

"You're welcome. So where do you call home?"

Grateful that she wasn't asking him a more awkward question, he described his home valley, from the peak of the mountain that sheltered the bay, to the small village that hugged the shoreline. He described the river that wound its way down through the valley from the lake, past the old abandoned mill. He even described the dump and was so wrapped up in the telling that he didn't notice the puzzled look on her face. Nor did he see the look of enlightenment when he described the houses on pilings

"I know that bay," she said. "It's on the other side of the island. Wouldn't you know it. Boy it's a small world. I have an old Auntie that lives in one of those houses and cousin Clarrisa is the Fisheries Officer. She has her office in one of the float homes."

Now it was Raven's turn to look surprised.

"Yes, I've met Clarrisa," he said cautiously. "What a coincidence. Now that you mention it, you have the same eyes"

Linda smiled. "They come from my mother's family. Clarrisa's mother was my mother's sister. You know most people just give an address, not a full blown description of the neighbourhood. Only a photographer or an artist would recite that much detail."

Raven was beginning to feel a bit uncomfortable as Linda began to recall her visits to the bay. Her enthusiasm was obvious. Just when it seemed she was going to ask him more awkward questions, she looked up and said, "Oh great, Dad's here already."

The man, the trio had seen driving the dusty old farm vehicle that passed them on the dirt road, strode through the door.

"Hi Linda. What's all this about rescuing that white raven. Caging him for good would be a better choice." Then, turning to Raven, he thrust out his hand. "Hi, I'm George. That your car I see parked out on the road? Thought I saw it this morning when I was driving home. Were you up at the farm?"

"Yes sir," Raven looked at George's hand and tentatively held out his own, "but no one was home."

The old man gripped his hand and gave it a shake, letting it go abruptly. "Had to take a trip over to Port Alice for supplies. Almost didn't see you, those narrow spoke wheels hardly raise any dust. Nice car though, reminds me of the one father used to drive. Still got the engine out in the barn, dunno if I'll ever get to restore her now."

Linda stood up from her seat, "Thanks Mary," she called toward the kitchen as she grabbed the water bottle from off the table.

Handing it to Raven she said, "Here, take your water, you can drink it later. Come-on Dad, we had better get going I only have about thirty minutes left for my lunch break. You guys can talk about cars later, we have a raven to catch."

Raven wriggled out from the close confines of the booth and nearly fell as he stood up. Linda smiled at his clumsy exit.

"Did you fall?" She asked. "You keep stumbling as if you're hurt. I did warn you, if you fell on those docks, we are not liable."

Raven took the bottle of water from her hand. "It's

nothing," he said, "really." Then seeing her look of concern he added, "Honestly. It just bends the wrong way."

And just to prove he was all right, he marched out the door and into the parking lot.

Once outside Raven risked a good look at the water bottle. On closer inspection he could see it was going to be another puzzle for the appendages at the end of his arms.

He had already discovered that most knobs turned easily, but the cap on this bottle seemed fixed somehow. There was a smaller knob in the middle that looked as if it should have a hole in it but it was plugged with the same blue plastic as the lid. Was he supposed to pierce it? Maybe he had to pry it off. He tried twisting it with his teeth.

Linda and her father followed him out the door, both giving him a very strange look.

George looked at his daughter and shrugged.

"Odd chap." Was all he could say.

Half afraid the bottle would burst, Raven stopped twisting the cap. He had even turned the bottle upside down, but the water inside just sloshed around teasing him from behind the layer of blue plastic.

20
The attack.

Neither Linda nor her father commented on Raven's strange behavior over the water bottle, as they headed across the parking lot toward the docks. The old truck sat parked at the top of the ramp.

"OK Dad," said Linda, I'll fill you in. Ray here was out photographing the old sheds, you know those really old dilapidated ones past the end of the commercial finger, and he spotted that white raven. He's apparently sicker than a dying dog and I guess he's covered in chocolate. That's going to kill him if we don't do something, not that I think people around here would mourn the loss."

"Well I've got a cage in the back of my truck here, plus a net, my bag and a tranq dart if we need it." He reached into the rear of the truck, pulled out a bag that he handed to Linda. Then reached back in and lifted out a large cage which he handed to Raven.

"Here lad, your legs are younger than mine. By the way, where's your camera? You might want to get some photos and we could use some good publicity shots to help raise funds."

"Ah well, that's it you see. I dropped it when I fell. It, . . . er . . . rolled off the dock and ah . . . sunk.

"What?" Linda spun around to face him. "You did fall. You're lucky you didn't sink along with your camera. You don't seem too upset. If that had happened to Dad, he would have been screaming murder."

Shock was also registered on the old man's face.

"You didn't have the strap around your neck?" He gasped.

"Uh . . . no, and . . . er . . . it wasn't expensive."

George looked disgusted. "Probably just one of those cheap, throw away digitals. You kids are all the same. You can hardly call that real photography. You can't even adjust the light speed on them things."

"Oh come on Dad, don't start in on the poor guy." Seeing the guilty look on Ravens' face, Linda rose to his defence. "Accidents happen."

"Yea but those docks are shaky. He could have fallen in at any time. Risking our necks just going out on them." And with that he turned and stomped off down the ramp.

At this time of year there were no sport fishermen in town and this section of the dock was empty. They turned toward the commercial finger where several large fishing boats were tied up. They were soon past them, with Raven leading them toward the old boathouses.

Raven signaled for them to be quiet.

"He can't see us from this angle," he whispered. "The last time I saw him he was up on the centre beam of that end shed."

George motioned for Raven to put down the cage. From the bag Linda was carrying, he pulled out a small oblong case. Turning to Raven he questioned "You said you got a good look at him, how big would you say he was? About the same as an average raven or bigger?" He opened the case and took out a strange stick made of metal and plastic.

"About the same size as me . . ." said Raven without thinking. Realizing instantly that he was no longer a bird he quickly corrected himself, "I mean my bag, ah, um . . . the one I left in the car . . ."

Then realizing he wasn't making much sense he added, "Ah . . . he's full grown. Does that help?"

Both Linda and her father were staring hard at Raven.

"Sorry," he said, "I guess the fall and losing my camera really did get me rattled."

Linda's father nodded, "Ok," he said, "that I can understand. I just don't want to kill him with too much dope, especially as he is already weakened. In fact I'd rather not use this at all. If he's still in the centre of the shed he could fall in the water, and then he would probably drown before we can rescue him. We'll just have to see. We may not have a choice if he is still up in the rafters."

He opened up another small box and pulled out a dart that he slid into the metal tube.

"Well, I'm ready. Linda you stay here with the cage and bring it when I call. Let's go Ray, you carry the net, but be careful where you tread. I don't want to have to rescue you instead."

With George following close, Raven crept forward down the finger. Reaching the back of the shed, they flattened themselves against the wall.

From where she stood watching on the dock, Linda giggled. "Dad's been watching too many of those cop shows," she muttered to herself.

George inched forward, turned, and peered through a crack in the wallboards of the shed. After the brightness of the open dock, it was not easy to see into the gloom. He could barely make out the shape of the bird on the centre beam but it certainly wasn't a raven, it looked more like a kingfisher. After a few more seconds, his eyes adjusted and he could make out a larger shape huddled in the far corner, wedged up against the planking.

"Good," he whispered to himself. In the raven's current position, if he used his dart gun there was a good chance that the bird would collapse against the wall and remain on the beam, or at worst, fall onto the walkway. Signaling Raven to stay where he was, George crept forward and around the corner of the shed.

White Raven heard the creaks and groans from the old dock and guessed there was something, or someone, approaching. He could feel his strength rapidly returning. It came in waves. Strangely, as the creaking came closer, the power increased. He felt his heart race, his skin tingled. He could feel the power. He felt powerful. He felt invincible.

When the kingfisher started chattering an alarm, he tensed his muscles. Fuelled by anger; he waited. A shadow fell across the open doorway; he waited.

When the shadow solidified into a person, he moved. With a horrendous screech, he threw himself off his perch with all the force he could manage, flew across the shed, and struck. His claws tearing at flesh and his beak penetrating to the bone, his emotions were a storm, uncontrollable. His pent up anger exploded in violent rage. His head, which up until now had felt full of water every time he moved, was engulfed in a full blown hurricane. The wave effect thundered up against his forehead and put him off balance. He fell sideways just as George raised the gun and fired. The dart missed the white raven, and embedding itself in the wall.

Sensing he was no longer in any danger, White Raven quickly regained his balance and with a loud cackle flew across the shed to land amongst an old pile of crab pots. He turned to face the door, gathering his strength. Revenge. Flapping his wings and feeling their power, he prepared to strike again.

Seeing George stagger, Raven leaped through the doorway and grabbed him by the arm just in time to stop him from falling blindly into the water. Blood was streaming down his face and into his eyes from a large gash in his forehead. His arms were bleeding and torn, where he had raised them to protect his face.

White Raven had regained his strength and Raven knew he had to act fast. If his brother escaped now, it would be harder to trap him a second time.

Putting himself between George and the white raven, he pushed the old man out of the shed. With Linda's father out of harm's way, Raven turned to face his brother.

Their eyes met.

In that instant, White Raven recognized the source of the unknown power. His mind raced. Those eyes, they were the same eyes that he had seen that very morning. Eyes that were strong and powerful; eyes that were in the head of a black raven.

In a flash of understanding, he knew the young man

---

facing him, on the opposite side of the shed, was his brother. His brother had transformed himself into a man.

Raven felt his energy draining. The weakness he felt when he had visited his brother earlier, wasn't from the brown. Somehow his brother was sapping his strength. If his brother came closer, Raven knew he would be in serious trouble.

An evil glint crept into White Raven's eyes, as the reality of the situation struck him.

What's good for one raven . . . he thought and transformed, feeling the full force of the power he wielded.

In a blink of a raven's eye, a second young man stood on the walkway between the crabpots. A burly youth, wearing grubby, off-white jeans, and a tattered, white Tshirt smeared in . . . chocolate? A lock of unruly white hair fell over the glaring red eyes. He laughed at the look of shock on Raven's face. Then, the hate-filled eyes reduced to slits, the laugh turned into a snarl, and White Raven took his first step toward his hated sibling.

Un-used to his height and body weight; unpracticed in the art of walking like a human, White Raven stumbled and reached out for balance.

Bile formed in Raven's throat and he reached for the wall of the shed to give himself balance. He felt dizzy, there was a tingling in his arms, and he struggled to maintain his human form.

He needs our help. His life force is draining.

I can see that. But we are not supposed to interfere.

Not interfere!? Is it not our fault there is a white raven.

We created him. We let him escape. Now you say we can not help our chosen? I am sorry but this has gone on too long.

To the far reaches of the black with you and your council . . .

Just watch me.

Abruptly the tingling sensation in his finger tips stopped and Raven felt a surge of . . . something strange. The last time he had felt this way was when he had helped the frog. A warmth spread through his body and he knew, instinctively, that he wasn't alone. He could feel a presence, a power, stronger than he had ever felt before.

White Raven sensed the flow of energy. He too could feel this new source of strength and he reached out for it. His greed was beyond reason, his eyes glistened, his mouth curled into greedy smile.

He leapt over the first rusty crab pot on the walkway as he to drew on the new source of power.

"Brother." He smirked as he lifted one foot and placed it on the rim of the next crabpot and leaned forward gloating. "It's been a long time."

As Raven backed away his eyes came to focus on the crabpots.

Circular metal rims: circles of power.

In a flash he knew what he had to do.

White Raven felt a sickening lurch in his stomach. The black cloud returned to his head and he found himself slumped in a tangle of fish netting and feathers.

The last thing White Raven saw, before weakness overtook him, was the cheerful face of the kingfisher looking down at him before she swooped out of the shed chattering the news across the bay.

Raven swayed, his balance seriously compromised. Transforming the rusty iron rings of the crab pots to copper had drained his own newfound strength. Even from this side of the shed he could feel the pull of the copper and the instant he had felt it, the unknown presence had left him. He needed to get out of the boathouse before his energy was absorbed completely and he too changed back into a bird. He staggered back through the doorway, almost bumping into George, who was still leaning against the outside of the shed.

Reaching to help George, Raven glanced back into the shed. The copper had worked; there was no sign of the white haired youth, or the clothes he'd been wearing.

Taking George by the arm, Raven guided the old man, around the corner of the shed and down the docks. Linda came running the minute she saw them.

"What happened" she gasped seeing the blood running down her father's face.

"The white raven had recovered. It attacked your father the minute he stepped into the shed." Said Raven. "I'm sorry, I didn't think he had the strength. I feel really bad, but I think this attack has seriously drained that vicious bird. He is laying slumped amongst the crab pots. If you move quick, you can cage him before he recovers and attacks someone else."

"Thank God he didn't get your eyes." Linda gasped as she wiped some of the blood from her fathers face.

"Stop fussing," George brushed her hand away. "It's mostly scratches. My old skin tears easily. If Ray is right, we need to cage that bird immediately."

Linda went to the shed and glanced in. Seeing the collapsed ball of white feathers, she sighed in relief. "Looks like dad's dart has gone into effect." She called back to the men.

Raven nodded, safer to let her think the drug had knocked White Raven out. "Take care." He called out.

Convinced she was dealing with a drugged bird Linda reached for the cage and, not being gentle, stuffed the ragged ball of white feathers inside.

"A cage is too good for you," she muttered, but at the same time she marvelled at the size of the bird; cleaned up he would be magnificent.

Seeing the white raven safely incarcerated, Raven continued to guide George down the dock.

The further away he was from the copper rings the safer he felt.

21
An Invitation

Back at the entrance to the
marina, a seagull watched as Linda hefted the
cage into the back of the truck. The white raven looked a
sorry sight, slumped in the bottom of the crate.
George pulled a first aid kit from under the driver's seat
and Linda cleaned and sterilized his wounds.

While she worked, George turned to Raven, "Thanks
lad. Another second and I would have been in the drink.
Strange, you know I could swear I heard another voice
in that shed. He must have hit me pretty hard but I

could have sworn . . . Ahh well," he shrugged "we'll nurse that bird back to health and we won't be releasing him any too soon. He has a mean streak in him. Actually, I can think of several raptor centres that would be glad to have him in their collection."

George waited as Linda finished bandaging his arm. "Well now that I can see again, I'd best be getting back. Need to get that bird cleaned up before the sedative wears off. You know, I really thought I had missed with the dart." George looked down at the slumped white raven, a puzzled frown creased his bandaged forehead. "I guess it fell out when he collapsed. No sign of it now."

He turned, opened the truck door, stepped up into the cab and started the engine. "Thanks again," he called out and, with a final wave, he drove out of the parking lot.

As Raven walked Linda back to her office, Linda turned to him. "Well, that's enough excitement for one day. I had better get back to work, I'm already late. Where are you staying? I get off at five. If you want, you can meet me here and come out to the farm for a bite of supper." She tried not to sound too forward, but you didn't get that many good-looking young men in town these days since the mill had closed.

"I haven't really decided yet, I thought maybe I would just camp down on the beach."

"At this time of year? The campgrounds are all closed. We don't open them till May. We do have a couple of worker cabins at the farm; you can bunk down in one of those if you want. Nothing fancy, but you're welcome to use one. Or there's Lucy's B & B just down Main Street, past the post office. I hear she cooks up an awesome breakfast."

Raven nodded. "Thanks, I'll see if she has a room. If not, I may have to take you up on your offer."

"So I'll see you at five." Linda called back over her shoulder as she ran up the steps to the locked office door which she opened and, with a wave of her hand, vanished inside.

Raven stood at the bottom of the steps, staring after her for several moments. Bilgat swooped low overhead and landed on the rooftop. The look he gave the raven was penetrating.

"I know, I know," said Raven, "time to go. I just wish . . . oh well." And, with a big sigh, he turned his back on the marina and walked up the hill to the waiting car.

A half an hour later, the old car pulled off the gravel road and settled down in the long grass; her resting place for the last thirty odd years. It hadn't taken much to persuade her to return to the dump, although, at the last minute, she had decided to stop, turn around and back in.

"I might as well have a change of scenery," she rumbled. "I was getting a bit tired of the same old blades of grass and rocks. At least this way around I can watch the comings and goings on the road." She sounded wistful; as if sorry the adventure was over.

The two eagles perched on the back of the passenger's seat also looked a bit dejected.

The raven however, perched on top of the steering wheel, looked pleased with himself. Life was good, better than good, knowing his brother was no longer a menace to society. The copper surrounding the farm should keep his brother in a state of confusion. Yes, Raven felt in an extremely good mood.

The drive back from town proved un-eventful, with raven allowing the car to remain in control. Bilgat and Farcry had joined him as soon as they turned off the highway onto the gravel road, demanding to know what was happening to the white raven.

"Is he dead?"

"No, just sleeping."

"What will they do with him?

"I doubt he will get his strength back again, but, if he does, they will send him to a place for caged birds."

"Caged birds!!?"

"Yes, caged birds, and to my understanding he won't fly free again."

It was late afternoon. The sun hung low in the sky. Linda locked the marina office, walked down the steps, and looked up and down the street. There was no sign of Ray, or his car. She glanced at her watch, shook her head, pulled out her cell phone and pushed a few numbers.

"Sorry Dad, looks like I've been stood up. You'd better come and get me after all." She listened, nodding her head briefly. . . . . . .

"Na, no sign of him and it's now gone five-thirty. Funny but I had a feeling he wasn't going to hang around."

She paused again, nibbling her lower lip, tucking a wisp of hair behind her ear. . . . . . .

"Ok Dad, see you in about twenty minutes."

She pushed a few more buttons and then put the phone back in her jacket pocket.

Movement above her caught her attention. A large black raven was perched on the edge of the gutter, staring at her.

"Not another raven," she muttered to herself, then laughed as the bird twisted it's head to one side as though listening. "Just don't get any bright ideas like your white brother, or we'll have to lock you up too. One ransacking raven is enough."

The last vestige of the setting sun bounced off the

bird's head and Linda noticed how the black feathers had a pink, blue and purple shimmer to them.

Just like Ray's hair.

Now, where did that thought come from? She shook her head, and gave a big sigh.

"I guess I am more than a little disappointed," she admitted out loud to the bird on the roof. "He seemed a really nice guy. A bit unusual, but nice."

The black eyes were intense and the jet-black head nodded.

She turned away . . . talking to a raven . . . what next? she thought, laughing to herself. It had been a very interesting day and, when she next spoke to her cousin, she would have quite a story to tell.

Raven was startled. How did she know he was my brother? He queried to himself.

"She didn't. She was just making an association of species. He's a raven, you're a raven." Bilgat landed on the roof.

"Oh." Raven sounded disappointed.

"Just wondered what you were doing. Farcry has gone back to his favourite tree and I've been checking out a small creek that runs into the bay. I've eye marked a couple of juicy looking fish, so, when you're finished here we can go back to the islands and have a nice relaxing supper and celebrate."

The thought of food brought Raven back to his senses. Lunch, now a distant memory, had not been very satisfying. A fresh fish head would be a big improvement, especially if it still had the eyes. With a powerful flap of his wings, he took off from the rooftop.

"Nothing," Raven cawed. "I'm not doing anything at all. Let's go and eat. You have no idea how easy it is for humans to ruin the taste of fresh fish."

Linda looked up at the two birds as they flew overhead. An eagle and a raven flying together was unheard of. Only in legends did the two birds tolerate each other. Realizing it was the raven from the rooftop, she was even more surprised that he seemed to be conversing with the eagle as they circled in unison, flying out over the docks and down the inlet.

The strange reply to her father's query on the white raven's size, popped uninvited into her head.

Her eyes widened and a small electric tremor ran up her spine, causing her to shiver. In disbelief, she watched until the two birds flew out of sight.

"Yes," she whispered to herself, "you are about the same size."

High above one lone spirit waited. He muttered to himself.

Well, that all went as planned . . . not.
You really cooked your goose this time.
You knew copper trapped our powers.
Why did you let him do it?
It won t be long before the High Council is aware one of us is missing.
Then they will realize the White Raven escaped and we did not report it.
Relax you said.
Well, you will be relaxing for a long time, trapped down there.
In a rusty old crab pot, no less.

The White Raven

About the author.

A successful water colour artist for many years, Sue has written books about her art, her travels and for her children. She arrived in Canada in her early 20's after marrying a young Canadian, and settled on Vancouver Island

Now living on the shores of Cowichan Bay, Sue draws on the scenery and life around her in her paintings and in her books. When not in her studio or pottering about the garden, she can be found relaxing on their boat with her lifelong partner, who's not so young anymore, along with a good book and their two dogs.

Other books by Sue Coleman

Fiction

The Return of the Raven
The Trumpeter Swan

Non Fiction

An Artist Vision
Artist at Large in Alaska
Artist at Large in the Queen Charlotte Islands

Childrens books

Biggle Foo meets Stinky
Biggle Foo becomes a Legend.

www.suecoleman.ca
Email Sue@suecoleman.ca

Distributed by : Pacific Music and Art
http://www.pacificmusicandart.com/